BRIGHTY
of the
Grand Canyon

by MARGUERITE HENRY

Illustrated by Wesley Dennis

SCHOLASTIC BOOK SERVICES
NEW YORK • LONDON • RICHMOND HILL, ONTARIO

Most of the characters in this story are real, and most of the incidents actually occurred. However, with the license often granted to writers, I have altered a few facts for Brighty's sake. — M. H.

 This edition is published by Scholastic Book Services, a division of Scholastic Magazines, Inc., by arrangement with Rand McNally & Company.

1st printing . . . . November 1967

Printed in the U.S.A.

To
Harold C. Bryant
Superintendent
Grand Canyon National Park

and

Ernie Appling
Uncle Jim's friend
and a cowboy's cowboy

CONTENTS

Brighty's World

A SHAGGY YOUNG BURRO LAY ASLEEP in the gray dust of the canyon trail. Except for the slow heaving of his sides and occasional flick of an ear, he seemed part of the dust and ageless limestone that rose in towering battlements behind him.

The sun had been shining fiercely on his belly and now began climbing up over his sides, then slowly up the canyon wall. But for a long time the rocks held their heat and the lone figure dozed on.

A ground squirrel peered out from a chink in the wall, watching a moment with friendly eyes, then dived back where it came from. A cottontail rabbit played hop, skip, and jump around him. But nothing disturbed the little gray lump, not even a nuthatch hammering away at a juniper tree.

It was the wind, an uprising current from the canyon below, that finally aroused him. It whirled up his nose and down his ears, tickling him awake.

With a grunting sigh he began rolling, and with each turn just missed falling off his ledge into Bright Angel Creek, hundreds of feet below. Now he sat up on his haunches, squirming his back against the rough, warm limestone. He gave a luxurious yawn and gazed at the opposite wall, as if in search of some creature like himself. But there was only rock, rising sheer and lonely to the sky.

He stretched his forelegs and then he was up, shaking the dust from his coat. Over the ledge a few spears of bunch grass grew in a crevice. He leaned out into space and cropped them, jaws swinging sideways as he chewed, while his eyes, from under their thatched roof of hair, looked out over his world. It was a world of rock piled up and up, layer on layer to the sky, and down and down to the Colorado River far below.

Slowly, as if balancing the weight of his great ears, the little fellow swung his head around to follow the winding river. His eyes suddenly fixed on a tiny white spot, and at sight of it he opened wide his jaws, swelled out his nostrils, and began braying: *"Yeeee-aw — yee-aw! Yee-a-a-aw!"*

Instantly the canyon took up the cry. South wall

to north and back again it banged and bounced the bray until there was nothing left of it.

The burro waited, listening. His ears probed the white spot as if to pull something out of it. There it was — an answering sound! A bellowing halloa, almost as big and brassy as his own. It set the little burro into action. Down the trail he plunged, zigzagging from ledge to ledge, ears flopping, tail swinging, hoofs toe-dancing the narrow path. Once on his way, a kind of momentum took hold of him and he fairly flew, rounding one cliff after another.

Time and again he crossed Bright Angel Creek, a foaming mountain stream that tumbled downward to the river. For yards and yards he walked in its bed, picking his way around the glossy boulders. But he neither drank nor played in the water.

Only once did he stop to study his goal. The white spot had grown to a tent, and nearby, campfire smoke was curling upward. Satisfied, he plunged on again, always traveling within sight and sound of the busy creek.

The afternoon was late, and purple shadows were spilling down the canyon walls when he came at last upon the source of the smoke. An old, old prospector with flowing white hair was piling driftwood on a fire. And beside the fire stood an iron skillet and a bowl of yellow batter.

A Stranger in the Canyon

STEPPING SOFTLY IN THE SAND, the burro sneaked behind the prospector and playfully butted him up from his crouching position. The old man spun around, his face lighting with joy.

"Brighty!" he shouted happily. "You li'l ole pussyfooter! You eenamost upset the batter, to say nothing of me, myself." He let the burro nuzzle his grizzly beard. " 'Tain't hay!" he howled with laughter.

He laid more driftwood on the fire, then turned and began scratching Brighty, starting with the scruff of mane and kneading down the dark stripe along his back.

"Feller!" he thundered above the river's roar. "You sure got an alarum clock in your head! Tan my hide if you don't arrive 'zactly at suppertime. It's flapjacks tonight, see? Got the batter all done. Ain't it nice and bubbly?"

The burro began nosing the batter.

"Oh no you don't!" The old man pushed the burro's face out of the bowl. "You just wait till I flap 'em. Me and you's goin' to celebrate tonight."

He spooned lard into the skillet, and while it was melting, pulled some blue-flecked stones from his pocket and held them under Brighty's nose.

"Sniff 'em!" he urged. "Sniff 'em good. Where they come from, they's more — a hull bluish-green vein o' the stuff. And if I could just find somebody to help dig it up, then me and you could pack it out."

The burro's ears swung back and forth, asking for more talk.

"Yup, Bright Angel, you and me's struck it rich. We've found us enough copper ore to last till kingdom come, and mebbe after!"

He took off his black hat and let the wind comb

his hair. "We'll call our diggings the Little Mimi, for my sister's gal. It's like this, Brighty," he explained as he stooped to pick up a fallen blue jay's feather. "My kid sister had only the one gal, Mimi, and she's crippled in the legs."

He stuck the feather in his hatband and smoothed it out. "Mimi's purty as an angel — eyes blue as lupine and curls the color o' wood shavings. Now, Brighty," he said, his face shining with plans, "with the money from the ore, we'll buy her a wheel chair so she can go scootin' through life like a butterfly."

He paused to add more lard to the skillet. "As fer ye, young feller, when the money rolls in, I'll buy ye all kinds o' doodads — a tinkly bell for your neck and a shade-hat with holes for yer ears, and some flea-shoo powder, and . . ."

Brighty wheeled around, looking, smelling, listening.

"Hey! Hark to me instead o' the night noises. It's just the river sawin' away at the rocks, or some old coyote tunin' up."

But the burro's ears were prying into the night and his breath snorting in his nose.

"Humph, don't hear a thing myself." The old man poured two mounds of batter into the skillet. "Could be our ring-tail cat sharpenin' her toenails on a piece of drift," he said.

And then all at once the prospector caught movement. The tall figure of a man loomed in the dark. He stalked slowly toward the fire, a dead beaver dangling from one hand.

"Reckon I skeered you," the man grunted. His voice sounded rusty, as if it had not been used for a long time.

The prospector stroked the burro's neck, trying to quiet him. "Brighty here told me you was comin', but I wouldn't believe him."

Motionless except for his fingers twirling the beaver, the stranger sized up the prospector. Then his eyes looked past him to the tent, where a pick and a pan stood outlined against the white canvas.

The sweet smell of hot cakes filled the air, and the old man dropped a third spoonful of batter on the skillet. "In the shock o' seein' a human being," he said, "I mighty near forgot to cook for three mouths 'stead o' two. Would you believe it, stranger, I ain't seen a livin' soul 'cept Uncle Jimmy Owen and Brighty here for upwards o' six month? I'm mighty glad to meet you."

He waited for a "Glad to meet you too." When none came, he went on, his hand still quieting Brighty. "My name's Hezekiah Appleyard, but don't nobody call me by that handle. What's yours?"

The stranger moved in closer. The firelight made

his small black eyes and black beard gleam, and it picked out the red kerchief around his neck and splashed red on his face.

"Name's Irons," he said. "Jake Irons, beaver trapper."

"Now that's what I calls a good, short, sensible handle," the old man replied. "Folks calls me Old Timer. When I first heerd it, I looks around quick to see if some old guy's behind me. When I see they's referrin' to me, my hackles riz up." He faced around to the fire and turned the hissing flapjacks. "I'm used to the label now. Fact is, I sorta like it. Makes me feel I'm a sure-'nough canyon man."

The hard black eyes were on the cakes.

"Ye needn't just stand there gawpin', Irons. Come! Share our chuck. It'll be kinda nice to listen to man-talk fer a change, though Brighty here's got a mighty sweet song fer a burro."

"Don't mind if I do." The stranger smiled, but only with his lips. His black beard parted briefly, flashing two gold teeth, very shiny.

The old man could not help admiring them. "I come down here to the canyon seekin' gold," he said, "but I guess gold ain't the onliest way to get rich."

The pin eyes gave the prospector a sly glance.

Then, going over to a flat rock, Irons slapped down the beaver and took out his hunting knife.

"Go ahead, skin out yer beaver," Old Timer said, "but don't ye flaunt the smell in front o' Brighty. He don't like hot meat — nor meat of any kind, fer that matter."

Jake Irons knelt in the sand, and with nimble fingers skinned the beaver, setting aside the choice bits of meat. Before anyone could say scat, a ring-tailed cat leaped up on the rock and made off with the liver.

"Ain't she quick, though!" The old man slapped his thigh in admiration. "Her name's Wait-a-minute, 'cause she never does. Oh well, ye still got the pelt, and that's what ye're after."

Muttering to himself, Jake Irons stretched the beaver skin, using stones to hold it in place. As he turned around he almost bumped into Brighty, who stood with hindquarters hunched, threatening to let his heels fly.

"Reckon he's just a mite jealous about sharin' his supper," the old man laughed. "Leastawise, that's what I hope."

Blue-Flecked Rocks

WHEN THE CAKES WERE RICHLY BROWNED, the old man stacked a plate for Jake Irons and handed him a jug of honey. Then he fanned a single cake in the air to cool, and sprinkled it generously with sugar. He smiled sheepishly. "Brighty likes sugar better'n honey," he explained. " 'Tain't so slobbery."

As the trapper watched, Brighty took the rolled pancake from the old man's hand and began chewing rhythmically, thoughtfully.

"You two always dine on cakes and honey?" Irons asked. The note of scorn in his voice was lost to Old Timer. "Only when we're celebratin', stranger. And now how about samplin' a cup o' my coffee? Uncle Jim says it's black as a thief's heart."

Jake Irons glanced up sharply, trying to read the old man's thoughts, but Hezekiah Appleyard was not even looking his way. Irons flashed an ugly grin. "I like my coffee black as that," he retorted.

The two men and the burro finished their supper in silence, while a handful of stars pricked holes in the sky.

After a while the old prospector took a gold watch from his pocket and began winding it with a little gold key. " 'Tain't but seven," he said, winding. "I'll pile more wood on the fire, and how about us chinnin' some before beddin' down?"

"Much obliged, Old Timer, but soon as the moon shines over the brink I'm crossing the river and heading up to the South Rim. By the way," he asked, making his voice sound casual, "what you celebrating?"

The old man held his tongue, thinking. He picked up a sharp-edged stone and began cleaning Brighty's hoofs, as though he could clear his thoughts at the same time. He failed to see that the stone he was using for a pick was veined with blue.

But Irons' quick eyes caught the telltale color of copper ore. His mind began racing. "Now, don't you bother spilling your secrets to me, Old Timer," he wheedled. "It's just like I said. I'm topping out of this black pit, and I don't figure to come back.

Not ever. I'm tired of trapping. Ain't enough beaver in these waters to keep me in grub."

The old man was only half listening. He was eyeing the lean hard body, noticing the sleeve stretched tight over the bulge of muscle, the big broad-fingered hands with their broken fingernails, the solid legs encased in their puttees.

"You mean ye're done trappin'? And outa work?" he asked.

"That's exactly what I mean. I ain't one to complain, but tonight's the first square meal I've had in weeks. And when I saw your cozy camp with the critter and all, right away I says to myself, 'Here's a man I can trust.' "

Old Timer looked all around as if to make certain they were alone. " 'If ye're really done trappin'," he cried, "mebbe you could work fer me! I need a young muscly feller, 'cause . . ." His voice pitched high as a boy's. " 'Causc me and Brighty's found an extry-ordinary vein o' ore."

Jake Irons smiled to himself at how neatly his flattery had worked.

"Yup!" the white head nodded. "With you and me to dig, and Brighty to pack the stuff out, us three can get rich quick. Y'see, I got a sister with a crippled youngster, and sick folks needs lots o' money."

"Yeah, I know," Irons said sarcastically. "You're just the kind to give the stuff away."

Mistaking the mockery for approval, the old man sat down, leaning happily against Brighty. "Ye'll do, Jake Irons!" His eyes were far away and joyous. "Ye'll do as a partner in the Little Mimi Mine."

For a long moment the muffled roar of the river filled in the silence, and somewhere down the canyon a coyote howled.

"Even by starlight ye'll see how rich the stuff is." Hoisting himself up, the old man moved nearer and spilled the blue-flecked rocks into greedy, outstretched hands. "Here! Study on 'em, feller!"

Over and over, Irons turned the nuggets in his hand. Then he made a wide circuit around Brighty and fed the fire, the better to see. "Where'd you find these?" he asked, trying to hide the eagerness in his voice.

"Well, friend, me and Brighty was dawdlin' along, loafin' and pokin' along down close to the Colorado, when we spied us one o' them horny toads."

"And then?"

"Then Brighty flips this toad over with his li'l ole mealy nose, and underneath — guess what?"

Without waiting for Irons to guess, the old man

went on. "There, underneath, was one o' them blue-green rocks. 'Twas only a broken-off lump, but I figgered where there's one, there's more."

"Yeah. Like mice."

" 'Zackly. And I looks up overhead and I sees some more o' this color in an overhang of rock. And me and Brighty fergits the horny toad, and I begins a-diggin' and a-diggin'. Got so feverish I hardly stopped fer meals. If it hadn't been fer Brighty bellerin' at sundown, I'd like to starved to death."

Jake Irons returned the nuggets and flopped down in the sand on the other side of the fire. "Lots of veins look good to begin with," he said, "but they pinch off to nothing."

"Ye're right. Most of 'em does. But not this one. No, siree! It got bigger and bigger the further I dug. Only jest today was I certain sure. Come mornin', I'll take ye in the tunnel and show ye." He pointed north. " 'Tain't far. Jest over there a piece. Wait'll you see the tree-ladder I built up to the tunnel. She swings out a bit over the river, but she's stout enough."

Jake Irons plucked at his beard, figuring a way to accept the invitation and seem casual about it. "I see you got a tent big enough for two," he said at last. "And it's been a long time since I slept out of the wind. Besides," he added, looking toward the river, "it'd be risky tryin' to cross on that cableway in the dark. Guess I'll stay till morning, anyway. But your burro," he hesitated, "does he hug camp all night?"

"Ye're durn tootin' he does! And it makes me mighty proud. Until I chanced on this-here copper mine, I had only two things I took a pride in — one was my grandpap's gold watch with the gold key to wind it, and the other's Brighty. Found the little feller runnin' wild along Bright Angel Creek."

"So you named him Bright Angel, him being so bright, I suppose."

"Yup. Only he weren't no Bright Angel at the time. Great horns, but he was a sight! Some porcupine had made a pincushion outa his face." The old man clapped Brighty's rump. " 'Member, feller? If I hadn't come along about then and roped ye and pulled out the quills with my pliers, ye'd have gone under fer sure."

Chuckling, the prospector turned now to Jake Irons. "Guess he was so hungry and hurted, he figgered I was his best friend."

Irons' eyes avoided Brighty, and he strove to keep the contempt out of his voice. "And so he's latched onto you ever since, I take it."

The white head nodded. " 'Cept for summertimes. Y'see, Irons, he's like a migrator-bird. Winters, he lives down here in the canyon where it's warm, and summers he hightails it up to the North Rim where it's cool. Y'know," he went on, leaning back against Brighty, " 'twas him that made the trail all the way up to the North Rim. And mind ye, Irons, that wall is so steep he couldn't go the short way; he had to zig and zag! It's over twenty-one mile to the top!"

The old man stretched his legs and dug his heels in the sand. "If ever you decides to top out north 'stead o' south, Brighty here knows the way. Don't fergit that. And if he's a mind to, he can pack a pick and pan as nice as you please."

"You don't say!" Jake Irons' eyes glinted in the firelight.

"But I do say! And what's more, Brighty knows character. If ever he out and out kicks a man, there's a man can't be trusted. Once when we went to town, Brighty near kicked a barber up on the chandelier. Next I heard about him, that haircutter feller was servin' time fer thievin'."

The trapper went over to feel his beaver skin, but his mind was listening.

"Now, on the other hand," Old Timer went on, "take Uncle Jimmy Owen up on the North Rim. Know him, son?"

"Just by hearsay," Irons answered. "He's the government lion hunter, ain't he?"

"Yeah. He's the one. Well, Brighty's got good reason to mistrust Uncle Jimmy because he smells to high heaven of lions, and anyone knows a burro hates lions worser'n work. But does he hate Uncle Jimmy?"

"Don't he?"

"Indeedy no! He sidles up to him to get his back scratched, same as he does to me. Like I say, Brighty knows character even when it's wrapped up in lion smell. Why, if'n I was to die tonight, Uncle Jimmy'd step right into my boots, fur as Brighty goes. Right into my boots!"

Irons sharpened his knife blade on a rock, thinking. He hardly heard the next words.

"Y'see," Old Timer was saying, "Uncle Jimmy understands, just like I do, that Brighty's a free spirit. Seems like he's got to be free to breathe."

The talk petered out and the fire burned low. Yawning, the two men went into the tent and settled down for the night, the old man on his cot, the young man wrapped in his blanket. Between them the big gold watch hung from the ridgepole, ticking the minutes away.

Good-bye, Old Timer

THE NIGHT WAS NOISELESS, except for the wind and the river. A few sparks gleamed in the fire, like fallen stars. Brighty edged closer to the dying glow. The sand felt warm and scratchy to his skin as he lay squirming on his back, his hoofs pawing at the chink of sky between the canyon walls.

After a time the moon showed itself, and gradually, very gradually, began whitewashing rocks and promontories. It whitened Brighty's belly too, and his nose as he lay blinking upward. At last he snuggled into the nest he had made in the sand. He closed his eyes and let sleep claim him while the wind played with his scraggly mane.

All night long the wind and the river went on about their business, sweeping down the canyon. Sounds came through Brighty's sleep — the voices of coyotes and foxes, and the occasional ringing sound of a rock tumbling from crag to crag. But all of this was canyon music to Brighty, and he slept on in the friendly darkness.

Toward morning his thirst awakened him, and he took off for Bright Angel Creek, a small gray shadow winding among the deeper shadows of morning.

There was burro-brush on his way, and he stopped to browse here and there until his thirst pulled him on to the chattering creek. He waded far upstream, up where the water flowed so clear he could see trout darting under the rocks. He drank his fill — not in one long draught, but a little here, then up the creek a way and another mouthful, until he was satisfied. Sometimes he stood quite still, letting the water foam and feather around his legs. But more often he got into a rough-and-tumble fight with it, pawing madly until he churned whirlpools and eddies. Then he stood over it like a victor, blowing and snorting as he watched the sand settle to the bottom again.

Bright Angel Creek seemed to flow especially for him, to quench his thirst and wash his feet, and to grow willows and grasses that stayed green for him, no matter what.

Morning passed. The whole day passed, while Brighty played in the creek and browsed along-side it. Only occasionally he clambered over the rocks and up the stern granite walls to get away from its gushing chatter. But always he hurried back, as to an old friend.

With the coming of twilight, however, the babble of the creek seemed idle nonsense. He felt a need for human company. Somewhere in the shadows far below a nice old man would be stirring biscuits or hot cakes. A hunger and a longing came to him, and he clattered out upon the rocks to a parapet that looked down on the campsite. There! He spotted the white tent, no bigger than a deer tail. He worked himself into a bray that sounded loud and clear. When the last echo had died, he waited, listening. But there was no answer.

He brayed again — louder, fuller — longer, and again he waited for the answering halloa. But again there was none. None at all. Only the echoes growing fainter and fainter, until at last they were swallowed up by silence.

Even with no answer, habit was strong in him. He had to get to camp. For the next hour or two he wound along the wayward course of Bright Angel Creek. At every turn he stopped to peer down at the tent. But tonight there was no smoke curling upward, no sign of life. He looked north toward the tunnel. He was close enough now to see the ladder climbing the vertical wall. It too was empty. Old Timer was neither going up nor coming down.

As Brighty reached the rift of sand on which the tent stood, his feet slowed, then stopped altogether. Muffled voices were coming from inside, and before he could sift them apart, the lion smell of Uncle Jimmy Owen filled his nostrils.

"How do you like that!" a strange voice said. "Consarn it all, Jim, only once in a coon's age me and you has a fishing spree, and what happens? Old Timer gone!"

"He's sure gone, Sheriff. And there's something mighty wrong here. Old Timer'd never leave his camp like this, and his watch still hangin' here. If he'd gone off to Flagstaff, he woulda taken it along and tidied the place. It ain't like him to leave in a hurry." Uncle Jim's voice sharpened. "Somethin's happened to him, sure as shootin'."

"You mean he's — killed, perhaps? Right under my nose?"

Brighty pushed the tent flap aside, only to face the muzzle of a gun.

"Sheriff!" Uncle Jim's voice was a command. "Save yer lead. It's only Bright Angel; you 'member him!"

And the next thing Brighty knew, a slight figure had darted around the sheriff and a pair of friendly hands were fondling his ears.

Uncle Jimmy Owen was a small-sized man, built wiry. He had sandy hair and a sandy mustache, and mild gray eyes that now looked full into Brighty's as if he expected them to tell him something. But all he saw was his own face mirrored in the black pupils. He placed his hand on Brighty's chest and gently backed him out of the tent.

"Brighty," he said into the big furry ears, "things look bad for our Old Timer."

A wind was blowing toward them, and Brighty sucked it in. A noise grew in his throat, grew into a crescendo of braying. He faced toward the tunnel, as if his calling could penetrate the darkness and pull the old prospector out of it.

"There now, Brighty; there now, feller," Uncle Jim soothed.

The sheriff's voice was full of annoyance. "Quit

talkin' to that burro and listen to me, Jim Owen." He pointed to the vertical wall rising behind the tent. "See that narrow scar in the rock? That might be a trail leadin' away from the tunnel."

Uncle Jim nodded.

"Well, I'm going up there to follow along and see where it goes. You stay at camp, Jim, and you better have your six-shooter ready. There may be a killer around here."

The sheriff strode off while Uncle Jim, with Brighty at heel, walked over to the remains of the fire. He picked up two cups near the ashes.

"Mark my words, Brighty, Old Timer had company for breakfast. These cups still have a swallow o' strong coffee in 'em." He nodded to himself as he picked up two sticky plates. "Now I reconstructs it this way. Some fugitive from justice knew thishere Grand Canyon is made up of hunnerts of little side canyons to hide in. But by and by he gets hungry, see? And tired o' livin' on fish. He smells camp smoke and vittles cookin'. And — well — you knowed Old Timer, Brighty. He'd share his grub with you or me or anybody! And prob'ly he couldn't help tellin' about that copper vein he'd struck. You knowed how trusting he was. Then this other feller —" Uncle Jim broke off as he saw the sheriff hurrying back.

"It gets worse and worse, Jim," the sheriff panted, swabbing his hat brim with his handkerchief. "There's two sets of footprints up in the tunnel, and Old Timer's pick and shovel lyin' there. Looks like someone was diggin' and then left in an all-fired hurry." His head went around on its neck like an owl's. "Now, if I was a criminal, where'd I hide?"

Uncle Jim shrugged. "The canyon's full o' hidey-holes. Figger it yourself, Sheriff. Two hunnert miles o' dens."

"All right! All right! And since you're so smart — if you was a sheriff, and you spotted a fresh-staked claim and the owner missing, how'd you go about solving the mystery?"

Uncle Jim thought a moment. His finger moved along the stripe on Brighty's back, then on the crosspiece over his shoulder. "If I was sheriff," he said at last, "I'd count on the canyon to trap my man. Ain't nothin' like a canyon to squeeze a feller in. The ravens hollerin' at him. And snakes stickin' out their tongues, and willows pointin' their skinny fingers, and faces in the rocks accusin' him." Uncle Jim stopped short. "Speakin' o' rocks. Sheriff, I'd like to be sure o' one thing."

He led the way down to the big river and began leaping from boulder to boulder, his eyes squinting.

"You're looking for clothing snagged onto rocks, ain't you?" the sheriff shouted, trying to keep up.

"Yeah."

"I already done that."

"Hey, look yonder!"

The sheriff followed Uncle Jim's finger to Brighty standing on the shore, shaking something black between his teeth.

As he came toward them, the men saw that the black thing was a hat. Brighty was snaking it along, playing with it, and suddenly a blue jay's feather loosened from the hatband and fell to the sand.

Uncle Jim bent down and picked up the feather. He took the hat from Brighty's mouth and carefully brushed it with his sleeve. He tried to hide his feelings, and then he gave up and buried his face inside the hat and wept.

"The Colorado River never gives up its dead," he whispered, too softly for anyone to hear. He stuck the feather back into the hatband and gave his own gray hat to Brighty to play with. Wordless, he tried on the black one. It was an almost fit. A little sweating of the temples, and it would mold to his head.

The sheriff stared into the foaming water, his eyes narrowed in thought. "But how did it happen?" he said to himself. "Old Timer wouldn't just fall in — not an old canyon man like him. No — it wasn't an accident." He paused, and his eyes traveled up the cliff to the ledge of rock running toward the mouth of the mine.

Suddenly he nodded. "I see it plain as day. Somebody must've pushed him into the river."

Uncle Jim wiped his eyes. "Good-bye, Old Timer." He touched the hat brim in salute. "And don't you worry none about Brighty." Then his face changed. A look of steel came into his eyes, and his jaws clenched. "Afore we die," he said, staring at a sucking whirlpool, "Brighty and me will find yer killer and even the score!"

The wind picked up his words and scattered them over the river, while the men and the burro walked toward the camp.

As soon as Uncle Jim entered the tent, he knew the killer was still in the canyon. Old Timer's watch was gone!

The Sheriff Learns a Lesson

ALL THAT NIGHT THE TWO MEN HUNTED in the dark recesses of the canyon, but there was no trace of the killer. At daybreak the sheriff came upon a collapsible canvas boat hidden under a cliff.

"I like to be quick reporting a crime," he explained to Uncle Jim as he pulled out the bulky bundle. "We can scoot across the river in this, top out the South Rim, and be in the state's attorney's office before dark. He'll round up a whole posse to help us. Now, Jim, some way we got to get Brighty across the river, so we can take turns riding him up the wall. Hiking down is one thing — hiking up, another."

Tired after the long night, Uncle Jim was searching Brighty for ticks, not because a few less would make any difference, but because he mourned Old Timer and there was a measure of comfort in doing something for his creature.

The sheriff sputtered as he began untwisting the ends of the baling wire wrapped around the boat. "Whoever used this last sure tied it up tight against the rats. Wish that burro could pick this with his big yella teeth, 'stead of just standing there grinning and getting his ticks squeezed."

Uncle Jim came to help, but the sheriff waved him away. "You forget I'm a canyon man too," he said testily, "and a sight younger'n you."

Once he had the wire off, he demonstrated his strength by opening up the small boat as if it were an umbrella. Inside were a pair of oars and a roll of wire and two life preservers.

"Here," Uncle Jim offered, "I'll help carry 'er to the river."

The two men scrambled down the rocks to the water's edge, carrying the boat over their heads.

Uncle Jim raised his voice above the river's roar. "She'll ship water unless ye soak 'er first."

"Delays!" the sheriff fretted. "Always delays! Should be up to Flagstaff now." He yanked off his boots and socks, and rolled his trousers to his knees. He pushed the boat into the water, tilting it to let the waves slosh inside and out.

Meanwhile Uncle Jim inflated the life preservers and Brighty stood sleepy-eyed, watching the river lick at the boat with its muddy tongue. A tattered puff of smoke blew across his face from Uncle Jim's pipe.

"Ye'd get acrost faster if ye swang over on that cage, Sheriff," Uncle Jim said. With the stem of his pipe he pointed to a wooden cage hanging from a single cable strung across the river.

"Not me!" the sheriff shouted. "I get dizzy in a little old tree hammock in my own yard, let alone riding in a swaying cage over the river." He wedged the boat between two boulders, then cupped his hands to his mouth to make sure he could be heard. "And I ain't taking no chances on losing you, neither! You know Old Timer's sister, and you're coming along so's you can c'roborate my story."

Uncle Jim cupped his hands too. "I can't! Teddy Roosevelt's comin' to hunt lion, and I'm headin' up the North Rim. Got to work my hounds."

"You *was* heading thataway," the sheriff yelled. "I'll see someone drives you around the rim to your cabin tomorrow, first thing."

Brighty, tired of the talk, started to walk away.

"Stop him!" the sheriff bellowed. "Stop him!"

Uncle Jim called out "Brighty" just the one time, and the shaggy head came around. He waited for Uncle Jim to catch up to him.

The sheriff came running too, panic in his face. "Jim, we got to have him for the trip up. We *got* to. Time's the thing."

The corners of Uncle Jim's mustache turned up. "Brighty don't want to go."

"Oh," the sheriff mimicked, "he don't, don't he?"

Uncle Jim shook his head. "He ain't never crossed this mad river, and ain't likely he'll take the notion now."

"Then how come he wets his feet in Bright Angel Creek a dozen times a day and won't cross the river even once?"

"Because he's smarter'n folks, that's why. Besides, he's a free spirit. No man can herd him around."

"Oh, you reckon not? Well, I say he's going across. See? No little old burro is going to fox me."

Brighty scratched his neck with his hind foot, looking absently from one man to the other.

"Here's how we'll do it." The sheriff faced around to see if the boat was wetting through. Then he barked out his directions. "Me and you'll row across, then you snub that wire around a tree on the other side. Whilst you're snubbing the wire, I'll row back with the tag end and tie it on Brighty." The sheriff rubbed his nose, proud of his plan. "And then I'll push him into the river, and you can pull on the wire and drag him across."

"It's a plumb silly idee, Sheriff. He ain't a-goin' to like it. See how his feet's planted in the sand? He's spoke his mind a'ready."

"Blast it, Jim. 'Tain't what *he* likes. Remember, I'm the law, and I'm telling you to hobble him so's he can't blow before I get back."

Uncle Jim reluctantly did as he was told. He took off his neckerchief and twirled it until it was no thicker than a cord of twine. He led Brighty to a little place where he could browse. Then he tied the burro's forefeet just above the fetlocks, half hoping he would kick and refuse to be hobbled. But Brighty stood calm and unruffled, even as the two men walked away and got in the boat and put out for the opposite shore.

The river was four hundred feet wide at this point, and swift in spite of the silt it carried. Brighty stared after the boat, watching it bob up and down in the brown foam, watching it head for boulders, then suddenly whirl around to miss them.

A lone, desolate feeling came into him as he watched. He was glad when the ring-tailed cat and her train of kittens came rubbing against his legs. He nosed them, sneezing into their fur.

A butterfly flew over his head, taunting him with her freedom. He scared her away with his ears and began eating the burro-brush, still looking on as the boat reached the swift center of the river and then the quieter waters on the far side.

No sooner did it touch the opposite shore and discharge a passenger than it swung about for the return trip.

Somehow Brighty seemed to know that it was coming back to seize him. Yet he did not fight his hobbles nor try to break loose. He stared with solemn, unblinking eyes, as if his mind were hobbled too. He tore off more brush, but only held it in his mouth, his eyes watchful, expectant. The boat rose and fell with the waves, now half lost in foam, now in full view. On leaping water it was coming to get him.

Now the sheriff stood up in the boat, poled it in to shore, pulled it up on the sand. He was coming toward Brighty, dragging a wire along behind, dragging it over the boulders. Now he was half running, a noose of rope in one hand and the tag end of the wire pointing sharp at Brighty.

And still Brighty made no move. Not until the sheriff was close on him, so close that he could hear him pant and see the shine in his eye, not until then did Brighty move so much as an eyelash. Then with a high snort that was almost a laugh he leaped into the air, bounding in his hobbles like a rabbit, bounding up over boulders and through brush until the knot in the kerchief loosened and he was free.

"Come back!" the sheriff's voice screeched. "Come back, you tarnal . . ." He stamped up and down, clawing the air.

But Brighty was freedom-bound, climbing up and up, a wild feeling inside him. And far away on the opposite shore, a spry-legged figure cheered him on.

A Free Spirit

BRIGHTY WAS IN A KIND OF GLORY. Released from his fear of the mad, sucking river, he climbed, flying. Each deep-drawn breath filled him with a pleasure so piercing he did a light-hearted buck over his liberty.

He noticed afresh the joys of his world — the mesquite shrubs dangling their sugary pods, the sweet pungence of sage, a water ouzel diving into the spray of Bright Angel Creek. "I'm free!" his hoofs beat time as he ascended. "I'm free! Free! Free!"

A hawk came swooping low over his head to snatch a plump chuckwalla lizard. But just in time the lizard spied him, scurried for the nearest crevice, slid in, and blew himself up to fit. The hawk wheeled, soaring against the reds and blues of the walls until he was lost in the distance.

For days Brighty savored his liberty. He had for company all the small creatures that scampered among the rocks, and all the birds that sailed the sky.

And then one twilight as he was loafing along his trail, something in the wind brought his head up. Mule smell! Camp smell! His laziness was gone. He threw wide his jaws and let out a whistling bray. To his delight, the echoes were not alone in their answer. Mixed in with them were answering brays.

He ran leaping in their direction. And suddenly, around an elbow in the trail, he came full upon the scene. Two mules hobbled, and two men building a fire. One of the men, squat and red-bearded, was eating a cracker with one hand and feeding the fire with the other. For an instant they all regarded each other, and then Brighty was snuffing noses with the mules and the mules were dancing in their hobbles.

The bearded man came slowly toward Brighty, offering what was left of the cracker. Brighty took a long whiff, and unable to resist the familiar smell, began lipping the crumbs from the man's hands.

"Look, Joe!" the red-bearded man laughed. "Tame as a dog! We can use him to pack our cameras and stuff."

"Sure thing!" Joe answered. "Our mules have been overloaded. I've known it ever since we left Jacob's Lake."

The red-bearded man could scarcely contain his glee. "This little gray mouse has walked — wham — into a trap! He's going to work!"

The men laughed loud and long over their good luck. "Now we won't have to unpack the mules every time the trail gets narrow," one said. "He can share the load."

"Great Scott, but he's husky! Bet he could carry two hundred pounds without batting an eyelash," said the other.

Brighty had a good supper of crackers and beans, and because he was glad to spend the night in company, he let himself be hobbled close to the mules. In the morning he was all meekness while the men loaded a pack on his back. But when it was strapped in place, he changed his mind about carrying it. The weight was all wrong — entirely too much on one side. And the bellyband pinched horribly. It was not only too tight, but much too close to his forelegs. In his dumb way he tried to explain all this by refusing to budge a step. He just stood, stupid-eyed and sleepy, his feet grounded to the earth like lightning rods.

But the men did not understand. They sweat and swore at his stubbornness, not seeing it was due to their own bungling. They broke off a willow whip and slashed it across his rump.

Then fierceness grew in Brighty, and the quick thought of freedom flashed through his brain. He reared into action, and before the men could grab him, ran to the babbling comfort of Bright Angel Creek. There he stood in its coolness, ears waving defiance. "What if I were to roll now?" they seemed to ask. Without waiting for an answer, he buckled his knees and plumped over on his side in the water. Something in the pack cracked.

"Yipes!" the red-bearded man howled. "My camera!" He plunged into the creek after Brighty. "You stumblebum!" he yelled, jerking Brighty to his feet and whacking him with a stick. "You catch up to the mules now and mind your ways."

Brighty not only caught up with the mules, he

passed them. Then he went flying up the gravelly trail. Never was he more sure-footed. In and out of the creek, leaping over boulders, over little cataracts, and with every leap his bellyband loosened to greater comfort. He could hear the red-bearded man bellowing after him, and then a lasso came whanging through the air. With a corkscrew twist of his neck, Brighty lowered his head just in time to see the rope whirl beyond and tighten around a bulge of rock.

He hadn't had so much fun in days and days. Another leap and another, and now he stood on a ledge, looking down on the men. Suddenly he let out all his wind, and with a wriggling motion of his body slid the pack forward, down his neck to the rock on which he stood. Then daintily he stepped out of the ropes and kicked the pack, sending it rolling and tumbling downward until it caught in a juniper bush.

Loud cries echoed up from the men, and into the quivering silence that followed, Brighty sent a great raucous heehaw.

Over the Rimtop

WAS THERE A WILDERNESS IN BRIGHTY that could never be tamed? A need for freedom stronger than the need for companionship? Day-times the canyon was all he wanted — winds rumpling his mane, birds whistling at him, and Bright Angel Creek talking and laughing. But sometimes at night a loneliness crept in, and he would bray to the winking stars, as if asking them to come down and play with him.

All winter long the world of the canyon was Brighty's world. Here in the inner reaches the weather was fine and the mesquite beans plentiful, and he roamed about, snug and warm. Up on the rim, however, the snow fell endlessly. It half buried the trees and then drifted partway down the wall, laying a thick fleece on the rocks. The snow line made a regular marker for him, a white fence that kept him within the canyon eight months of the year.

But this year, with Old Timer gone, the canyon was not the snug hidey-hole it used to be. It seemed a dark, broody place, a wilderness of tumbled, jumbled rock. The wind cried and the creek blatted monotonously. Even the birds seemed depressed and kept their twitters low.

Often Brighty wandered back to Old Timer's camp. But once there, he drew into the willows. He was like a man in ambush, seeing but unseen. Day after day he watched the man, Jake Irons, climb the tree-ladder and disappear in the black mine like a mole into his run. And once he watched him climb down with a load on his back and swing across the river in the wooden cage. Then for a long time he could make out the figure crawling up the wall on the other side until it blended with the limestone and was lost.

As days came and went, a restlessness grew in Brighty, an urge to leave the lonely canyon. Now the sun was striking down a little earlier each day and staying a little longer. Its warm rays revived him, stirred him to the remembrance of the North

Rim. Up there a little alpine meadow lay cupped in the Kaibab Forest, and nearby was his secret cave with its pool of delicious spring-fed water.

Each day the stirring within him sharpened. His eyes kept gazing up at the rim, as if mere looking would melt the snow and hurry the spring. And then all at once it came. Warm rains washed down the face of the north wall, and when Brighty glanced up one early May morning, the white fence was gone.

Now he was like a man squaring his shoulders for a big job, a job he liked doing. His loafing days were over. He had some place to go! His summer home, big as the sky, was waiting for him up there beyond the canyon rim, and Uncle Jim would be waiting too.

He started climbing the miles as if there were no time to lose. He plunged into the rushing waters of Bright Angel Creek, almost strutting over the boulders. A willow branch whisked across his ears, bending them backward. Other days he would have taken time for a second rub, and a third, but today he hurried on.

Crisscrossing the creek was the trail he had made. He sniffed his way along, nostrils quivering in excitement. He caught the fresh scent of deer tracks, but it did not tease him off on little detours. Today, first things were first. Climbing was the thing! He paid no attention to a canyon wren scolding him, or to butterflies doing figure eights over his head. Resolutely he wound and twisted his way up and up. The prickly pear and hedgehog cactus reached out with their prickles and hooks, but nimbly he side-stepped them. Today nothing must stop him.

By noon he reached Ribbon Falls, a white jet of water that shot gaily out of the rocks above, washed down the face of a jutting ledge, and then joined forces with the creek. Brighty could never resist the pretty beckoning finger of Ribbon Falls. In spite of his hurry, he took a little cut-off trail that went behind the cascade. Memory led him to the place where the water divided around a boulder. It made a peephole just big enough for his head, ears and all. Shivering with pleasure, he poked his nose through, letting the spray tickle his ears. Memory, too, told him not to waggle them, for one flick to right or left and the force of the water would flatten them to the roots. He stood there awhile, showing his teeth in a burro grin, enjoying the peephole as if it had been made to size, especially for him.

Then back to the climb. And now the wall rising sharper and the trail spinning finer, and the little gray figure moving on, ears flopping, eyes unimpressed by the vermilion pillars on one side and the black abyss on the other.

Climb a hundred paces. Rest and blow. Climb. Blow. Climb. Blow. Try running in little dashes. Up toward a new voice — the distant voice of Roaring Springs. Listen to the growl, hear the hiss and howl. Then, deafened by the roar, see the chutes of water come spurting down the craggy rocks.

Blue shadows of afternoon, and now the hardest climb of all — the Devil's Backyard. Rocks, rocks, everywhere, as if some giant devil had ground his teeth and spit and spewed them in every direction. Smooth rocks. Jagged rocks. They scraped Brighty's shoulder. They blocked his feet. They made hurdles to trip and hinder him. But not even the rocks could stay him. He squared off, charged pell-mell up the boulder-strewn steps until the Devil's Backyard was behind.

He paused a moment, breathing heavily. At last the stiff climb was over! Ahead, dark evergreens and white-trunked aspen grew on either side of the trail. He was almost there, almost to the top of the world. A buck deer stood in his path, then made a whistling noise as he turned tail. With a joyous snort of his own, Brighty broke into a gallop and took out after him, crashing through the tangle of grapevine and scrub oak. Blue jays screamed at him. Squirrels scolded and scattered.

And then! And then! He was over the top, on the

rimtop of the world! Gone were the cliff walls and rock temples. Here was forest so dense it swallowed up the deer.

Brighty ran soundlessly on the forest duff, weaving in and out among the pines and aspens. And just at sunset he came upon his little cup of meadow nestled deep in the woods.

It lay in a pool of shadow with only slivers of gold where the sun pushed through the trees, and it smelled of the sweetness of lupine and wet earth and new grass.

With tired feet Brighty tested the welcoming green carpet. His hoofs sank deep. He doubled his legs like a jackknife and fell into its softness. A great peace came over him. For a long time he lay still, as if bedding down for the night. Then wanting to feel more of it, he began rolling blissfully, this way and that, enjoying the springiness of the grass after his rocky canyon beds. At last he rose to crop the juicy blades. A doe and her spotted twins came to share his retreat, but they gazed wet-nosed at him from a little distance.

The sun dipped low and purpled the shadows across the meadow. Brighty heaved a sigh. The meadow was just where it should be. He had rolled in it. He had eaten his fill of it. Now to find his secret cave and then to give himself to sleep.

The Fight in the Cave

AN EERIE MOON DANCED ITS BEAMS along the threadlike path from Brighty's meadow to his cave. He stopped a moment to listen to the stillness of the night, but he found that it was not still at all. A bat whirled around him, squeaking, and an owl whispered, "*Who, who, whooo?*"

With a grunt of happiness, Brighty loped along the path until it opened out into a black cavern. Here nature had built a vast shelter with an over-hanging cliff for a roof, a wide sand-swept floor, and one side open to the canyon. But what endeared it to Brighty was the pool of clean, clear water near the back wall, and the bed of ferns to lie in.

Tonight the moon quicksilvered the pool, and as the droplets fell from the cracks in the ceiling, they made the water wrinkle in an ever-widening circle.

Brighty's keen eyes looked around his lair, and his ears pricked to catch the small, dulcet notes of the water. They had not changed their tune—*Plink, plash! Plink, plash, plink!*

He buried his muzzle and drank deep. Then he settled down in a clump of ferns like a tired child come home at last to his own bed. His mouth opened in a great stretching yawn. Everything was just as before, even the ghost-white tree trunk guarding the open side of the cave.

As he lay among the ferns, watching the sailing moon, there was a sudden uprush of wings and a great flock of doves swept into his grotto. The noise was deafening. But in spite of it, Brighty's eyelids drooped as he let the doves share his pool and scratch in the sand, eating the grains. They left as noisily as they had come, and no sooner were they gone than a mule deer stole silently to the pool to drink. But Brighty had already fallen asleep, his little snorings blending with the windsong and the water tinkling into the pool.

Night wore on. The wind died. There was only the *drip-drip* of the water, and a fern stem teetering back and forth to Brighty's breathing.

Then from far below the lip of the cave a mountain lion came slinking upward, her tawny coat mixing with the lights and shadows of the rocks. Her cat eyes gleamed golden-green in the dark as she crept nearer and nearer the old dead tree. She halted there a moment, then hooked her claws into the trunk and climbed swiftly until she was even with the cave.

At first Brighty lay undiscovered in the darkness. But the lion's eyes prowled the shadows and suddenly fixed upon his white belly. For a long time she seemed bewitched by her prey and lay watching him, her tail lashing, her mouth partly open, showing the white fangs.

At last she stole soundlessly forward on a limb, tested it with her forepaws, then with her whole body. It bent to her weight, and she steadied herself, balancing like a diver. Then, with one powerful leap, her body made an arc in the blackness.

At the very moment of her leap Brighty was snuggling deeper into the ferns, and she landed short of her mark. Cruel claws, intended for his head and neck, ripped his forelegs from shoulder to hoof. Instantly he was sharp awake, a fire of pain shooting up his legs. He leaped to his feet, squealing in terror as he faced the howling, hissing lion. He pawed wildly, kicking at her fireball eyes, trying to push her over the brink.

But cunningly she rolled underneath him, cuffing

and stabbing with rapier claws. Brighty backed away, rearing, then came down, flailing with his hoofs. Once he landed on the soft, muscly body, but she slithered out from under him. He could feel blood oozing hot down his forelegs, but he felt no weakness. Only a frenzied need to stamp out the yellow flame of her eyes, to stop the hissing sound.

Suddenly the lion turned, and with a bound was up in the tree. She tried a second spring for the catch, and this time she landed on Brighty's back. Down they both went on the floor of the cave, a snarling, grunting shadow in the moonlight. One moment they were almost in the pool; the next on the rim of the abyss, with nothing but darkness and space below.

The stars swam around Brighty and mixed with the moon, and his blood trickled darkly in the sand. He tried to shake free of the claws stabbing his shoulder, but they only dug deeper. Now the two figures grappled and came again to the pool, and they were spinning into the icy water. Still the lion would not let go. With a scream of pain Brighty rolled over on his back, pinning her beneath him in the water. For long minutes he held her there. Then gradually the claws eased, and at last they fell away.

Curious First Aid

All the next day Brighty lay in misery. He kept biting at his cuts, trying to quiet the throbbing, but the gashes only widened and the burning pain ran up his legs. He moaned tiredly, and from time to time sank into a half sleep. He was too weak to eat, and he would not go near the tainted pool to drink.

Night came again, with the whirring thunder of the doves. And then sunrise, with hummingbirds drinking of the droplets as they fell. Out of the weary fog of his mind Brighty saw a spry-legged figure enter the cave, heard a familiar voice cry, "Brighty! Bright Angel!"

A wave of memory swept over him. He tried to fix his eyes on the little man wearing a black hat, but the whole figure rippled like something under water. Even the voice had a tremble in it.

"Brighty," Uncle Jim was saying as he stared at the hoof marks and claw marks, "you must've had a mighty tussle!" In an instant he was on his knees, gently parting the blood-matted hairs, examining the wounds. "These rips is bad, feller, mighty bad, but I'll pick us some globs o' pine gum and make a quick salve. We'll soon take the burn out o' them angry cuts."

As he stood up, he looked for a moment into the pool. "Whillikers!" he whistled. "A *big* cougar! She's six feet or more! 'Pears to me ye wrestled her into the water and drownded her. How'd ye do it, feller?"

Brighty's eyes watched the little man as he made a cup of his hands to catch the dripping water. It wasn't a very good cup. It leaked. But still it held enough to feel cool as it went down Brighty's throat. He closed his eyes while his ears flicked to remembered sounds — twigs being broken, and after a while fire crackling. Then came the pungent sharpness of pine tar in his nostrils.

"Now, boy," Uncle Jim explained while he poured the resin into Brighty's cuts, "she may hurt a leetle, but I *got* to do 'er."

He bent over the burro and began working the salve into the open sores. "You had me uneasy as an old biddy hen," he went on. "The warm rains come and the spring flowers, and I says to myself, 'Bright Angel'll be here next, any day now,' but ye didn't come and ye didn't, and then I commences to fret and stew, and finally I set out to hunt ye."

The thick, warm fluid did not hurt at all; it felt soothing. And the voice of Uncle Jim was something to hold to, like a rock in floodtime. Brighty let out a great sigh of relief, and lifted his head a bit as if life were good again.

Uncle Jim stood up, and suddenly he was regarding his overalls as if he had never noticed them before. "I've an idee!" he crowed, eyes twinkling in triumph. He took out his pocketknife and pierced the denim just above one knee. Then he cut his way around the pants leg and stepped out of it.

"Y'see, boy," he said, "if we hide yer cuts, ye can't pick at 'em so easy, and they'll heal nice and clean." He began cutting off his other trouser leg, chuckling to himself as he worked. He stepped out of that too.

"Lemme see now, what was invented afore buttons?" He thought a moment. "Why, pegs, o' course!" He broke off several twigs and sharpened each to a fine point. "We'll jest peg yer pants on!"

Next he laid his own bright red suspenders on Brighty's shoulders and slipped the pants legs over the tiny hoofs and up the torn legs, taking great care to hold the cloth away from the wounds.

"How about that!" he exclaimed, pegging the suspenders in place. He stood back, admiring the effect. "Now ye'll feel better, boy. Just ye rest a bit whilst I see about what's in the pool."

Brighty sniffed the old blue denim and felt a strange easing. He stretched his legs out stiffly and sat up on his haunches, watching as Uncle Jim hauled the heavy body of the lion from the pool. After he had removed the paws, he dragged the carcass to the lip of the cave and with great effort flung it into the chasm. From out of nowhere three ravens came cawing and swooping down after it.

"The only good lion's a dead 'un!" Uncle Jim said, scrubbing his hands with sand.

He fastened the lion's paws to the trunk of the dead tree, and painstakingly carved the name

"Brighty" into the bark. "In all Arizona," he said, "I figger there ain't another li'l ole burro smart enough to kill a cougar. Ye deserve a marker."

It was a strange-looking pair that left the cave and slow-footed toward Uncle Jimmy Owen's cabin on the edge of the meadow. But there was no one to see the old man with his cut-off pants showing two white legs bowed as powder horns. And there was no one to see the shaggy burro limping along after him, his pants legs swinging like a sailor's bell-bottoms.

No one to see? No human beings, that is. But everywhere wide, unblinking eyes stared — the eyes of deer and cottontail rabbits, and squirrels and grouse and jays.

There was no visible tie rope between the man and the burro, but it was there all the same — a tie rope of such stuff as could never thin out and break apart.

On the Mend

WHILE BRIGHTY'S WOUNDS HEALED, he grazed, stiff-legged, in Uncle Jimmy Owen's meadow. He saw little of Uncle Jim during the day, for in all the Kaibab Forest no man was busier. Hunting parties came to Wiley's Summer Camp nearby, rough and rugged men, eager to hunt mountain lion. And it was Uncle Jim who served as their guide. He fitted big men to big mules and little men to little mules. And besides hunting, he lent a hand when things needed doing at Wiley's Camp.

But nighttimes belonged to Brighty. Then he was the center of things and everything happened around him. Uncle Jim came home to him — came home riding a white mule with a train of riderless mules behind him, and a pack of yelping, footsore hounds.

Brighty went limping each night to greet them, braying a lusty "Welcome home" as he went. When the mules had been fed and bedded down and the hounds cared for, he would nudge Uncle Jim toward the cabin.

"Sure tickles me, Brighty," Uncle Jim would laugh softly, "the way ye hustles me along. Seems like I'm yer critter, 'stead o' the other way around."

While he prepared supper over the cookstove inside, Brighty waited outside in nervous eagerness, pawing and stomping the earth. Then after supper he tailed Uncle Jimmy from one Ponderosa pine to another as he gathered yellow lumps of resin.

"You'll make 'er!" Uncle Jimmy would say every night as he melted the gum and stirred it with his finger. "Yup!" he would nod, pouring the warm gum into each gash, "soon you'll be going lickety-larrup again. What's more, yer hair'll grow long enough so's hardly a scar'll show."

Brighty always sat for this performance, his tail stretched along the ground behind him like a piece of rope. He enjoyed the whole business of having his wounds dressed. He even got into the habit of lifting one forefoot and then another, stepping into the pants legs like a child trying to dress himself. As for the suspenders, he was growing used to them too. They gave with every motion, and rubbed pleasantly across his shoulders at an itchy spot he could never reach himself.

"Git along with ye, Brighty!" Uncle Jim pronounced when his nursing was done each evening. "I got my cabin to tidy up."

Brighty loped off then to tend his own business. There was a big chunk of red salt inside the mule corral, and by poking his head between the rails he could get a good lick at it. He had worn a sizable trough, and always his tongue grooved the same place, licking, licking in slapping rhythm. Meanwhile the white mule worked on the other side of the chunk, as if trying to meet Brighty halfway. It was a routine they went through every night.

Afterward Brighty walked all around the corral, cleaning up wisps of hay that the mules had let fall over the fence.

Not since his fight with the cougar had he slept in his cave in the mountain. He was content to hug the meadow, where he could hear the mules snorting and the comforting noises from the cabin —

Uncle Jimmy singing cowboy songs and dumping the dishwater out the door, sometimes just missing him by a hair.

One night, instead of cooking supper over his stove, Uncle Jim built a fire out-of-doors. Brighty watched big-eyed, watched the sour dough being pinched off into mouth-sized pieces and laid in a neat pattern in the Dutch oven.

"Bet this minds ye of Old Timer, don't it, Brighty?"

The burro sidled closer, asking to have his back scratched. With a floury hand Uncle Jimmy obliged. "Lucky thing no womenfolk about," he said. "They'd squeak like mice at my cookin' and scratchin' yer lousy li'l self all at the same time."

Brighty leaned his weight against his friend, enjoying the moment.

"What women don't know," Uncle Jim confided, "is that a flea'd ruther cling to a passel o' fur than a bald biscuit! Eh, Brighty?"

A grunt came in reply.

"Sometimes it 'pears to me I needs yer company a sight worser'n ye needs mine! Daytimes I'm too busy to mull about things, but when night comes my mind fastens on Old Timer and I gets a sad, pinched-up feeling."

He paused in his rubbing and took off Old

Timer's hat, looking at it as if he could see the white head of hair and the twinkling blue eyes it used to shade. "We ain't forgot ye, Old Timer," he said. "It's just that yer killer's so slippery. We know he's hidin' somewhere in the canyon — prob'ly just waitin' to take over yer mine." He turned now to Brighty, an angry light in his eyes. "But me and you'll round 'im up if it's the last thing we do!"

A night moth settled on the black hat, and Uncle Jim flipped it away. "Money don't mean a tinker to us, Old Timer. A reward's been offered fer the villain, but every cent'll go to help little Mimi. Ye'll see."

This night when supper was done, Uncle Jimmy did not go off gathering pine resin. He took out his knife and slit open Brighty's frayed pants legs. Then he threw them into the fire. A black smoke curled upward and the smell of pine gum filled the air.

"Thar, partner!" Uncle Jimmy said, his voice suddenly grown husky. "Ye're free! Free as that night bird wingin' out over the canyon. Go on, feller, take off!"

Brighty looked down at his bare legs with the new hairs covering his scars, and let out a wild braying! He struck off for the corral and high-stepped around it like some show pony. Then back he came at a gallop, sliding to a stop in front of Uncle Jim.

The man laughed, and then he felt a little glow of pride rising in him. "How often," he asked, his eyes on the fire and one hand working hard at his mustache, "how often do I got to tell ye, feller? I ain't one to hang onto ye! Good-bye, Brighty. Ye're free!"

But Brighty lingered. It seemed as if he wanted to square accounts for the long weeks of nursing. One early morning when Uncle Jim came out of the cabin carrying his water tins, Brighty blocked his path, almost asking to be put to work.

Anyone else might have brushed the little fellow aside with a laugh: "Yeah, I know. Ye'll run off with my tins and I'll waste the hull day trackin' ye."

But Uncle Jim thought a second, and his eyes lit up with pleasure. He went into the cabin for a shoulder strap and then packed the tins on Brighty. He started up a path to a small spring on the hillside.

While he trudged on ahead, he rummaged in his mind, trying to find some reason for the change in Brighty. "Mebbe," he mused to himself, "it's like what happened to that kid who had to have his hair shaved off. Straight as string it was. But when it growed back after the fever, I'll be danged if it didn't kink out all over his head — like tendrils on a morning-glory vine.

"Mebbe," he concluded, "some critters changes character after a sickness, 'stead o' looks. Now ye take Brighty's fight with the she-lion. Could it of been a settling influence on his character?"

Uncle Jim faced around to make sure that Brighty was following. Yes, there he was, head bent to the climb as if fetching water was the prime thought of his life.

The old man nodded, answering his own question. "That's the way I see it."

He sighed a little as he took the tins from Brighty's back and plunged one after another into the spring. "Feller," he said shaking his head, "I'm mighty obliged for the help, but don't ye get too domesticated on me!"

The Lion Hunt

AS THE SUMMER DAYS PASSED, Brighty became Uncle Jim's steady companion in all his work. By and by he actually went on lion hunts.

One cool, bracing morning in late July, the very air seemed charged with expectancy. A heavy dew had drenched the earth, and lion scent promised to be sharp and clean.

Everyone was eager to be off — Uncle Jim and his hounds, and Brighty and the mules. But most excited of all were the special guests, President

Theodore Roosevelt and his tow-headed son, Quentin. They had come all the way from the capital city for Quentin's first cougar hunt.

Just as gray dawn gave way to sunrise, the party took off. Brighty alone wore a warning bell, as he was the only animal young and tender enough for lions to attack.

"Ah!" the President exclaimed as the company jog-trotted out of Uncle Jim's meadow. "This is the way to live. Close to earth and sky." Then he chuckled. "With a dash of danger to give it spice!"

There was no need for answer. Everyone was feeling the bigness of the morning — hounds whiffing and carrying their tails well up, pack mules stepping out on a slack rope, and Brighty capering in the dew, as if this were the morning of the world.

For a mile or so they wound through the forest toward the canyon rim; and as the trees gave way to thicket, the youngest hound began yipping and running in circles.

Quentin cantered up alongside Uncle Jim. "Lion?"

"Nope," snorted Uncle Jim. "Rabbit!" Then he wheeled his mule, and with Brighty helping, drove the overeager pup back into the pack.

Uncle Jim, as he rode, flung little pebbles that

struck the earth a mere inch or so behind the hound. "Less'n I have a nosebag of li'l bitty stones," he called to Quentin, "one o' the youngsters goes kitin' off on rabbits and upsets the hull pack."

With the pebbles to remind them, the hounds settled down to lion business in earnest, their noses lower than ever. They fanned out as they moved through the underbrush, scenting cold trails too old to puzzle out. And they came in again. And they scattered until Brighty was bewildered, not knowing which to tail.

It was well toward noon when Old Bones, a bluetick hound, bayed the news that he had found fresh lion scent.

"Hear 'im! Hear 'im!" Uncle Jim shouted to the pack.

With a rush, the others hit the line behind Bones and broke out in full cry. Their voices rang quivering in the air, and the very melody made Brighty's blood quicken.

Instantly he was on his toes, flying with the pack, pounding along the forest duff, dodging tree trunks, jumping fallen logs, galloping along the rim. He could hear Uncle Jim whooping and hollering behind, and the air gone wild with hound music and mules snorting and hoofs beating. And under his chin his own tinkly bell adding to the tumult.

Suddenly, in the rimrock ahead, the tawny body of a full-grown lion leaped from a tree and disappeared over the rim into a tangle of scrub oak. The pack was after him, a screaming stream of bodies, diving into the cover.

Although the brush was heavy in shadow, Brighty, trotting along the rim, could see their tails waving him on. Their cries, too, stirred him with excitement. To him the hunt meant but one thing: keeping pace with the hounds or, better still, setting pace! He saw ahead a notch in the rim and flew toward it. And now he was scrambling down the notch through spiny undergrowth, picking his way carefully. All the while the hounds were coming along toward him. Now to outsmart them!

Breath snorting in his nostrils, he skidded down the steep red cliffs, almost sitting on his haunches. He landed on a little shelf of rock that ran along the wall several hundred yards.

As he minced along this ledge, he was enjoying the three-way race — mules and men on the rim, hounds lower down thrashing through the cover, and lower still he, Brighty, tittuping along, sending little stones spitting into space.

Meanwhile the mountain lion kept to cover, gliding through the close-growing oak on thickly padded feet. He ran with stealthy, flowing step, and the color of his fur was one with the sand and the shadows.

Minutes passed, and more minutes; and just when the scent seemed hottest, the lion shot from cover, up the rock layer parallel with the hounds. For a few yards he dashed forward, then dropped again into the thicket.

The hounds, baffled, broke out too, casting themselves in and out of the underbrush, trying to regain the scent. Up on the rim Uncle Jim cheered lustily, yelling to each by name. "You own him, Bones; go away with him! Hunt him up, Warbler! Try on, Possum! Go into 'im, Younker and Whiffet!"

His cheering was magic. Old Bones pushed on and hit the line again. With a shrill cry, he voiced his find to the rest of the hounds.

Brighty had no thought but the fun of the race. He did not see the big cat now heading for a yellow pine in a hollow, now climbing up the trunk like a lineman up a telephone pole. He was conscious only of hound music, wild and shrill, and that he was leading the pack, dancing along his ledge loose and free, his bell sounding his own excitement and joy.

Up in the pine tree, right up in the open sunlight, the lion glanced from side to side. His enemies were closing in. On the rim above, the men with rifles ready; behind him, the panting, blood-hungry hounds; and far below, the yawning chasm. But near below, his cunning eyes spied a gray creature traveling with the wind, his back a safe landing place.

As a fish leaps when it is hooked, so the cougar made one stupendous leap. He landed with a thump on the burro's back, and the jar drove Brighty to his knees. Then he was up, bucking in terror as he fled, trying to shake loose his fearsome rider. The ledge was narrowing into the face of the cliff now, and he tried to scrape the lion off before they would both go hurtling into space. He tried again, a desperate bucking and a scraping, but the weight was still there.

And now the ledge tapering finer and finer, and death riding on his back and rocky death below, and his blood beating with the powerful urge to live. He wheeled on his hind legs, and his forelegs went clawing up the bare wall toward the patch of cover. Above him three rifles pointed and three bullets pinged the silence as a mass of fur and fangs and claws went mushrooming into the briar. Almost at once a lasso whirred through the air, encircled its thrashing prey, and pulled the great beast to the rim, the hounds yelping behind.

Brighty shuddered his coat to make sure he was rid of his burden. Except for the stinging scratches on his neck and shoulders, he found he was not really hurt. So with a happy grunt he went bounding up to join the mules and the men.

The President and Quentin, and Uncle Jim too, made a great fuss over him, as if he were a hero come home from the wars. No one could tell whose bullet it was that had killed the lion, but each of the hunters secretly felt sure it was his own.

When Uncle Jim saw that the claw marks on Brighty's back were not deep, he busied himself skinning and butchering the cougar, throwing a piece to each of the hounds. He talked while he worked.

"Fear instinct, I'm thinkin', is what told Brighty to come toward us 'stead o' leapin' into the abyss. But now, gentlemen, if he'll pack this skin, then he's a hero sure 'nough."

The President and Quentin stood silent, watching while Uncle Jim used his knife with quick, sure strokes. When he had loaded the meat on the pack mules, he rolled up the hide and tied it with a thong.

"Now, don't ye do this if'n ye ain't a mind to,"

he said to Brighty. "If ye're frighted o' the lion smell, you just skedaddle and I'll hoist 'er up on my ole mule."

Brighty took a whiff of the skin and seemed to know that now it held no danger. He stood transfixed, letting Uncle Jim lace it on his back while Quentin stroked him and whispered into his ear.

The President was mightily impressed. "You're game, Brighty!" he exclaimed, looking into the quizzical brown eyes.

"Ye're durn tootin' he is, Mister President!" Uncle Jim agreed. " 'Tain't easy to pack yer enemy dead *or* alive. I kin see his heart tappin' to double time and his nose hatin' the job. But he'll do 'er!"

That evening the party made camp in Brighty's grotto at Cliff Springs. Freed of his burden, Brighty hung back at the entrance, standing with the hobbled mules, watching Uncle Jim throw down the bedding and build a fire to cook supper. Then, as no one urged him, he haltingly stepped inside. He went over to his pool, sniffed all around it, and at last drank deep of its mountain freshness.

Everyone was in fine appetite, the men and the hounds eating lion steak, which the President pronounced as delicious as venison. Brighty, however, preferred the frijole beans.

After supper the hounds settled around the fire,

licking their cuts, while the two men and the boy sat in a semicircle, facing out across the chasm. Brighty joined them, sitting as one of them.

The slanting sun was at work on the opposite wall of the canyon. It looked as if some giant painter over on the South Rim had mixed all his reds in a bucket and tipped it over the brink, spilling liquid fire down the rock layers.

The spectacle put an awed silence on the men. But as the color dimmed, there was talk of many things. The President confided his dream of making the Grand Canyon a National Park. And Uncle Jim told him how fine a thing that would be; then badmen wouldn't dare hide in the side canyons, for there would be too many visitors nosing about.

As the shadows deepened, Uncle Jim began at the very beginning and recited the murder mystery of Old Timer. When the story was done, Quentin leaned forward. "But you've *got* to find the killer, Uncle Jim. You've *got* to!"

And the President's voice rang strong with conviction. "Don't you give up, Jim! In my book, the scales of justice eventually come to balance."

The cold night wind was rising now. Uncle Jim fed the fire, and as the flames lighted the cave, the President took a notebook from his pocket and began writing.

"What are you saying, Father?" Quentin asked.

"Just a moment, Son." And he wrote on.

When he had finished, the father handed the notebook to the boy, who read aloud in his clear young voice:

> The canyon fills one with a sense of awe. Under the naked sun, every tremendous detail leaps into glory; yet the change is startling from moment to moment. When clouds sweep the heavens, vast shadows are cast, but so vast is the canyon they seem mere patches of gray and purple and umber. Dawn and evening twilight are brooding mysteries over the abyss. Night shrouds its immensity, but does not hide it. And to none of the sons of men is it given to tell of the wonder and splendor of sunrise and sunset in the Grand Canyon of the Colorado.

Brighty's ears forked to the singsong words. They had a nice chime to them, but he hugged to Uncle Jim all the same, his eye on the dead tree trunk, remembering.

Brighty Goes to Work

THE NEXT DAY THE PRESIDENT AND QUENTIN left for Washington, and life settled back into routine. But Uncle Jim felt concern about Brighty. Was he becoming a plodding pack animal, forgetting his wild ways, his memories of freedom?

Uncle Jim decided to make a test. If Brighty would go to work for someone else, then it would be plain that all the wildness had drained out of him. What about young Homer Hobbs? he thought.

Homer was the waterboy for Wiley's Summer Camp. He was a gangly youngster with brown, doelike eyes and arms too long for the rest of him. Though a shy one with people, he had a pet deer and a skunk and a grouse, and he seemed easy and at home with animals.

Uncle Jim made a point of arriving at the spring one morning when he knew Homer would be fetching water. "Homer!" he exclaimed as he caught up to the boy. "Mebbe Brighty'd pack water fer ye too."

Startled, the boy looked around, his brown eyes gleaming with interest. "Y'mean," he hesitated, "I could have Bright Angel part time?"

"Mebbe. Who knows? He's getting to be such a workaday feller, he might just be glad to help a neighbor out."

Homer's shyness was suddenly gone. He looked straight into Brighty's eyes and then into Uncle Jim's. "I'd like that," was all he said.

" 'Tain't every man I'd loan him to, but even though ye're only crowdin' 'leven, ye're Cal Hobbs' son, and ye come by yer knack with animals nacherel. I swear I don't know what's got into him. Ever since he kilt a lion, he's tame as a lamb."

It was only a matter of days before Brighty was

dividing his time between Uncle Jimmy's place and Wiley's Camp.

There was a handful of children at the camp, and Brighty enjoyed their generosity. Every time he gave a child a ride, he was rewarded with the most delicious treats — licorice sticks or cherry drops or slightly squashed cookies. Sometimes it was a juicy apple. And so before long Brighty was hiring himself out as a child's mount. Of course, he went where and when he pleased and at whatever pace suited his fancy. But his gaits were so remarkably smooth that children took to riding with their arms outspread.

"Look, Ma!" they would shout. "No hands!"

But let some grownup climb aboard to show the children how to ride, and Brighty turned demon. At the first kick to his ribs he took off like a bird. Then in midflight he suddenly put on the brakes. The luckless man always flew over Brighty's head and landed like a frightened goose in front of him.

Brighty's second-best trick was an about-face. He would be loafing along, head down, as if half asleep. Then, without any warning, he would wheel and gallop off in the opposite direction. The unfortunate rider never seemed to make the turn with him, but to go forward into space, quite often ending up in a spiny bush. To make matters worse,

Brighty had a way of looking back over his shoulder, showing his teeth in a wide grin.

With Homer Hobbs and the children, Brighty was meekness itself. But he seemed allergic to grownups. Once when Homer went to town on an errand, a stout, red-faced man took over his job as waterboy. He brought out the tins and began to sharpen a pine twig with his knife. Brighty's eyes rolled knowingly. Quickly he backed up, screening himself in a little grove of aspen. There he stood, motionless, his white nose matching the white bark and his eyes like the black boles.

The man cupped his fat hands to his mouth and shouted, "Brighty! You come here!"

When the burro did not come, the man stormed into the aspen grove and whacked his way through, the pine stick almost touching Brighty's tail.

"Consarn that fool jack!" he sputtered. "Where *is* he?"

The madder he got, the more he yelled. And even though it was barely sunup, the children, some still in pajamas, came running out of tents to see what the noise was about. A sharp-eyed little girl spied Brighty and nudged her friends. They broke out in snickers at first, then they howled with mirth.

"You kids tell me where he's at!" The man lurched around. "And be quick about it!"

For answer they only whispered behind their hands and laughed the louder.

This threw the man into a rage. A second time he strode into the aspen grove, and again passed right alongside Brighty, while the children's laughter mounted beyond control.

It was one thing to be outwitted by a burro, but being laughed at by children was more than the man could bear. Snatching up the water tins, he stamped off toward the spring, muttering as he went.

An hour later he returned puffing, his face purple with exertion. And there, coming to meet him, was Brighty, wide-eyed and innocent. In anger the man threw one of the tins at the burro, who dodged as artfully as if it had been a rock slide on a canyon trail. Then he hightailed it for the meadow.

Later, when the man strode over to Uncle Jim's to tattle on Brighty, there was just the hint of a smile on Uncle Jim's face as he listened. "Now, ain't that a fine way to do!" he said in the tone of a parent whose boy had smashed a window. "I'll have a talk with Brighty about this."

But when the man was out of earshot, Uncle Jim slapped Brighty's hip in relief. "Praises be!" he laughed. "If ye'd answered to the proddin' stick, I'd sworn the world was comin' to a no-good end!"

Within the Black Tunnel

SUMMER FADED THE INDIAN PAINTBRUSHES, and the grasses dried so that there was little taste left in them. Nights grew cold, and laid a breath of hoarfrost on the meadow. Brighty took to sleeping in an old cliff dwelling, where he could nestle into the dry leaves that whirled in through the opening.

But as the weather sharpened, mountain lions often left their tracks close to his sleeping place, and coyotes and wolves grew bolder. And when one day Brighty's whiskers were iced by the moisture of his own breath, his mind began pulling him toward the canyon. Down there the wind would blow warm over his body and the sand would scratch him pleasantly, and there would be water running night and day, with never a skim of ice on it. Suddenly he seemed driven to leave the rimtop, and he started out, his feet hurrying him toward his warm winter home.

As Brighty went by the cabin, Uncle Jim happened to glance out the window. He was standing at the table pouring a cup of coffee for the sheriff, who had come to pay him a visit, and he stopped with the cup only half full.

Puzzled, the sheriff followed Uncle Jim's gaze. "Rope him, you dang fool!" he said. "Don't just stand there google-eyed!"

Uncle Jim put down the coffeepot and hurried to the door. His hand rose to his mouth and he started to call out, but something made him change his mind.

"Good-bye, feller," his lips said. "I'll be seein' ye again . . . when the lupine blues."

He stood silent in the doorway, watching Brighty step lightly along, head nodding, ears flopping. He watched until the small gray figure was swallowed by the forest gloom. "Who kin rope a wild, free spirit?" he asked with a little burst of pride.

The sheriff let out a snort. "Humph!" he exploded. "Who'm I to say? I can't even rope a killer I know is crawling somewhere in the canyon. It's been ten months since Old Timer was murdered, and I ain't found the killer yet."

All that winter Brighty roamed the inner reaches of the canyon alone. Sometimes, when the wind was still, he thought he heard voices like his own on the mesa across the big river. But soon the wind would strike up and the voices would be lost in it.

Snow fell again on the rimtop and sifted down, building again the white fence, penning him in the canyon. No human beings angled down his trail, and the days drifted by like slow-moving clouds.

One day toward spring, when Brighty was skirting the snow line, he took a notion to make a trip all the way down to the Colorado River. Just as day was breaking he set forth.

Bright Angel Creek tumbled over the rocks and babbled to him as he went along. The noise it made shut out the rumble of thunder, and he felt the small rain on his nose before he saw it. At first it was not much more than a splash. Then there were more splashes, scattered here and there in the dust of the trail. By and by the drops smalled, coming closer and closer together, and then the fury of the storm suddenly let loose! Great inky clouds rolled down from the summits. Lightning flashed in yellow veins, joining crag to crag. Thunder roared. And torrents of water spilled from the heavens.

They sluiced over Brighty's head and funneled into his ears. They spouted down the hairy watershed over his eyes.

The wind worked with the rain, blowing and battering at him, then swirling a gray curtain around him until it was too thick to see through. He slipped on a rock and fell to one knee, while the rain pummeled him and seeped through his hair and into his skin. He scrambled up and went groping blindly, letting his feet see for him, letting them feel their way along.

Some homing instinct seemed to guide him, for all at once he found himself on a ledge leading to the Little Mimi Mine, and then he was ducking his head in and under the rough-hewn entrance of the black tunnel.

A stench rose to his nostrils, not just of foxes come and gone and their droppings left behind, but a man smell that pulled a trigger in his mind. Except for the rain, he would have fled from the smell, but he was cold and wet and the tunnel was warm and dry. He wriggled in, and suddenly felt two human hands striking at his chest. They were trying to push him out of the tunnel onto the rocks below.

With a startled scream, Brighty struck down with

his head, hitting the man's head. It made a dull echo in the tunnel. He sledge-hammered again and again, until he felt the hands lose their force.

As he came on into the darkness, he could sense the man backing away, keeping distance between them. The tunnel was quiet now, except for the rain gushing down over the entrance. But away from the rain he heard a smaller sound — a steady ticking sound that he remembered. He sank to the floor in exhaustion, listening.

All that night there was no letup to the storm. It loosened boulders and sent them crashing down the cliffs until the floor of the tunnel quaked.

Brighty slept fitfully, waking to the rockslides and to his hunger gnawing. A sour-dough biscuit was flung in his direction, but it smelled of dead beaver and he only nosed it.

With the morning, the rain petered out and a murky light filtered into the tunnel. It outlined the figure of a man, and what he was doing touched off a small, sharp message to Brighty. He was winding a shiny gold watch with a gold key.

Caged over the Colorado

THE WIND BLEW IN LITTLE GUSTS into the tunnel, and worked through the dampness of Brighty's coat. He felt the chill against his skin and shivered.

The man mistook the shaking for fear. "Hah!" His voice made a ghostly whine in the tunnel. "You're scairt. You're no angel. You're a scairt devil. And I can whop a scairt 'un."

Stooped like some monster ape, he advanced slowly toward Brighty, long arms dangling below his knees. Brighty stiffened. He did not dare edge out of the tunnel backward; it would mean falling to his death. He turned around. But the dark hulk leaped at him, and with a sudden motion flung a belt around his neck. In panic, Brighty tried to toss his head free, but the ceiling of the tunnel was too low. He felt the belt buckle jerk into place and saw gold teeth grinning at him. Then a hard flat hand boxed him across the ears.

"Now, you bony broomtail," the ghostly voice said, "I'll break that sassy free spirit of yours!"

Planting himself against the entrance to the tunnel, Irons unwound one of his puttees and made a cinch around Brighty's barrel. He tied two heavy bags of ore to the cinch and then stood back, coldly eyeing the weighted figure.

"You came just like I whistled for you. With two bagfuls of samples to show in town, I'll find grub-stakers a dime a dozen. And now, broomtail, the law'd never look for a man to cross the river on a day like this. Eh?"

He got behind the burro, pushing. Anxious to get away, Brighty ducked his head and came out of the tunnel onto a narrow sill or rock.

Terror caught at him. The river had risen until it nearly reached the sill. The cottonwood ladder had been washed away. He and the man were standing on a ledge that was no more than a scar in the face of the cliff. There was only one way to go. The sill of rock led to a catwalk, and this in turn led to a browlike platform where a cable spanned the river, carrying the cage to the opposite shore.

Brighty, with the man following close behind, made his way up the cliff. His pack scraped against the wall at each cautious step. The storm tore at him, and only the anchor of heavy ore held him to the narrow trail until he came to the platform.

Below him he saw the river heaving boulders from its bed, grinding and crashing them together, and tossing along whole trees with roots upturned like bony arms waving for help. The wind was in league with the river, whipping the cable back and forth, shaking the cage like some wildcat with its prey.

Jake Irons seemed to gain power from the elements. With great long sweeps of his arms he worked the cable, pulling the cage in toward the platform.

At sight of the oncoming thing, Brighty reared up on his hind feet. But the man was cat-quick, grabbing him, choking him with the belt while the cage went hurtling back to center. With one viselike hand on Brighty, he ripped off his shirt and tied it over the burro's head as a blindfold. Then with savage strength he worked the cable again, bringing the cage back onto the landing. His eye measured the width of the gate, and quickly he took off Brighty's packs and loaded the bags far forward on the floor of the cage. Then he shoved Brighty aboard, let down the slats, and climbed on top to work himself and his captive across.

As the cage began zooming down the cable, a wild dread seized Brighty. He couldn't see. He couldn't breathe. He flung his head up, grabbing the shirt in his teeth, biting it, ripping it open. And then in a flash he saw he was boxed in a tiny, barred prison. The prison was more to be feared than the river! He kicked wildly at the bars, but only a few splintered, and the wind carried them off like matchsticks. There is no knowing how Brighty wheeled around in that tiny space, yet he did, and with a mighty leap he was over the gate. But the belt around his neck caught on a stud post, and there he hung, suspended over the river, his body thrashing wildly to free itself.

Up on his perch Jake Irons clung to the framework in desperation, trying to keep from being pitched into the current. His legs hugged the bars, and his frenzied hands fished for a knife, found it, and slashed Brighty's neck strap where it hung on the post.

With a mighty splash, Brighty fell into the river. His body sank for a long moment while the raging waters wrenched off his cinch and swirled him around and around. He struggled against the waves, but cruel eddies kept pulling him down. He tried to keep his nose above water. He gulped for air. It stank with the odor of dead fish, but he sucked it into his lungs and felt his body rise. He gulped again. He swam a stroke or two, and again drew in the foul air. A floating limb struck him across the neck, then glanced off as if it had met its match.

He grappled and swam his way toward a boulder, clawed for footing; but it was slippery with mud, and he slid back into the water. Now the river was driving silt into his coat, weighting him down, and weariness was heavy in him too.

On the bank he saw a lone beaver eyeing him forlornly. How far to that shiny eye? Two breaths away? A dozen? He fixed on the eye as on a goal and swam toward it, against the brown flood and the driftwood. Wave after wave slapped him down, but his body seemed made of rubber, bouncing up to the surface again.

Maybe it was that shiny eye pulling him up out of the river, guiding him like a beacon. Or maybe it was his great lungs developed in climbing canyon walls. Whatever it was, from deep within, Brighty drew one mite more of strength. And now he was scrambling up on the beaver's rock, gasping for air.

When his sides stopped heaving he shook his coat, spraying water and mud over his furry little savior. Then he tossed his head. The neck strap was gone! He shook his body to make certain the cinch and the bags of ore were gone too. Yes, he was free! And back on his own shore! He showered the beaver again and sneezed when the little fellow returned the favor.

The Battle Scars o' Freedom

THE NARROW SHORE LAY WET AND SNAGGED with uprooted trees and broken rock. Brighty wanted to roll, but there was no room. It was the wind that finally dried his coat. It chilled his body, too, so that he shivered violently. Yet a fever burned in him and he was hot and cold at the same time. The beaver had long since deserted him and he felt lonely in the wind.

Finally he crumpled into a little heap among the drift and fell into a heavy sleep. Black night came, and gray morning. Stiffly Brighty got up, and his gaze climbed the north wall until it met the sodden sky. Where was the white boundary of snow? Where?

He blinked solemnly under his hairy eyeshade. It had been there the last time he had looked — a solid fence of white. Now it was gone, and up yonder, up over the rim was refuge! He tried his legs, and they moved woodenly over the masses of drift, moved slowly toward Bright Angel Creek.

Today there was no friendly babble to the creek. It was angry and dirtied by the storm, and Brighty floundered across it, struggling against the rushing current. His trail, too, was spoiled. New rock piles and twisted trees got in his way as he shuffled upward.

The shaking came and went, and he could hear his breath whine in his lungs.

Toward noon a warm April sun came out, steaming the rocks and drying the slopes. Exhausted by the constant crossings of the creek, he stopped once to rest and roll in a patch of sand that fringed it. But instead of a nice tingly feeling, he noticed only that the sand got in his nose and throat, and the cough that followed hurt deep inside him.

He climbed in sun and in shadow, picking his way over gooseneck roots, over rock slides. Another day he would have stopped to explore any change in his trail, sniffing excitedly and pawing it with his feet. Now he felt only the need to find the voice and hands of Uncle Jim.

He climbed blindly on, stumbling often; but always some unseen force lifted him bodily and on he went, his stubby legs working up and up the wilderness of cliffs. A cactus spine hooked into his ankle, but even pain did not stop him. His head low, he trudged with all the power of his will; and when he coughed, it blew the dirt ahead of him.

He passed Ribbon Falls and Roaring Springs without so much as a look-up. It was his hoofs he watched, one ahead of the other, inching their way up the path that twisted back on itself like the wriggling of a snake.

All day he went without drinking, until at last he saw tiny cups of snow in the timber beside the trail. He wet his lips in one cup and another. Then he lifted his feet again and limped on until he was over the rim. No bucks or does or little spotted fawns were there to welcome him.

Slowly, silently, he moved along the forest aisle to Uncle Jim's meadow. The sun was dipping down over Buckskin Mountain when he finally looked through the window of the cabin. Uncle Jimmy, with a pup in his arm, was feeding it milk from a spoon. Brighty tried to bray, but the sound that came was the merest sob. He watched sickly while the feeding went on, and then he was seized with a fit of coughing.

Before the spasm was over, the cabin door flew open and Uncle Jim, with the pup in his pocket, stood squinting at his miserable, mud-caked visitor.

"Brighty! You?" he whispered in unbelief. He walked around the dejected creature, examining him on all sides.

"My poor li'l ole hermit," he said, "wearin' the battle scars o' freedom." He lifted Brighty's foot and felt the ankle swollen from the cactus spine. "Ye sure been a target fer trouble."

The pup, forgotten, began a shrill yipping which was answered by all the hounds in the kennel.

"Dang it!" Uncle Jim sputtered. "It's so noisy around here a feller can't hear hisself think. Ye wait, Brighty, whilst I put the pup to bed in my old wool sock. Then I'll bring ye bottles and brews, and we'll lick yer troubles. Ye wait now."

Brighty closed his eyes. He had no intention of doing anything but wait. He must have dozed off, for when he woke with his coughing, there was Uncle Jim at his side.

"This blanket weren't made for no li'l bitty burro," he was saying. "It's mule-size!" He took a fold in the middle and pinned it in place with safety pins. Next he found two flat stones, and using them as tweezers, pulled out the cactus spine in a fraction of a second.

"Thar!" he said. "One thorny in the flesh is gone!"

Brighty did not even flinch. He let the gentle hands feel the puffiness around the sore, let them wind a bandage around the ankle. "Learned this trick from Old Timer," Uncle Jim said, talking as he worked. "First ye wraps the festered place like this, and then ye pours a strong brew o' tea on the bandages. And by and by it draws out all the pizen."

The tea sloshed over Brighty's foot. He sniffed the aroma, and a violent spell of coughing came on that made Uncle Jim reach for the bottle marked "Liniment."

With firm strokes he rubbed the liquid on Brighty's throat from ear to ear. "Hot, ain't it? And guaranteed to make yer circulation flow fast as the Colorado."

Brighty snorted at the smell, curling his lip.

Uncle Jimmy laughed. "I plumb forgot how ye hates even a mention o' the river." A sudden thought struck him. "Could be ye got doused in it?"

Brighty's head was nodding with weariness.

"Wait!" Uncle Jimmy said. "Jest one more smidgen of medicine, and then ye kin doze to yer heart's content." He whittled a piece of wood in the shape of a paddle and poured a mound of thick brown cough syrup on it. Then he pulled out Brighty's tongue and plastered it with the syrup. "Now then," he commanded, "swaller! Quick-like!"

Brighty fought the medicine until it slobbered out of his mouth, staining the doorstep.

"A fine how-de-do!" Uncle Jim said. "Same stuff as I give to Teddy Roosevelt years ago when he taken cold. Name me another burro what ever got a taste o' President's medicine. Fer shame!"

Uncle Jimmy measured out another dose, but Brighty clamped his teeth and turned his head.

"All righty. You win." He screwed the cap on the bottle. "I'm thinkin' ye had enough doctoring fer now, anyways. And maybe sleep's the thing."

Some of the medicine had spilled on Uncle Jim's hand, and he licked it up with his pink tongue. "*Peeeeuw!*" he said, and spat the brown stuff as far as he could. "Grasshopper juice couldn't taste bitterer. No wonder the President's a great man. Anybody what'll down this will down a heap o' things and come up big teeth a-grinnin'."

He pulled the blanket close around Brighty's neck, pinning it tighter. Then he gathered up his bottles and brews, and laid them quietly in the basin. He waited until Brighty's eyelids closed before he tiptoed into the cabin and shut the door behind him.

Silence filled the twilit meadow except for Brighty's harsh breathing and the wind rustling the tiny new leaves of the aspen trees.

The Carrot Cure

FOR BRIGHTY, the days followed one another in a dull sameness. All around him there was the blue of lupine and the pink of spring beauties, and meadow grass showing green. But he looked out of film-covered eyes, and his days were gray.

The festered place on his ankle was healing clean. It was the cough that persisted. What hurt Uncle Jim was the way Brighty's head nearly touched the ground when the spasms came on. And the sound he made was a kind of croaking, like an old man dying. It was worse at night, and penetrated Uncle Jim's sleep so that he tossed and turned on his bunk, wondering what to do.

When he awakened one morning, he pulled on his corduroys instead of his overalls and made a beeline for Brighty. "I'm goin' to town," he said, "fer two reasons. One is, I promised to see the sheriff, who's heard talk of a badman hidin' out in the canyon. But the prime reason is to buy me the tools that'll get cough-mix down yer gullet, or my name ain't Lion-killer Jim!"

He pulled his handkerchief out of his pocket and wiped the corners of Brighty's eyes. "Sometimes inside o' me," he said, "I get skeered, almost. I don't like the way yer eyes is scummed over and runny."

As Brighty watched Uncle Jim ride off on his white mule, the meadow was suddenly unbearable. The silence shrieked at him, and the trees seemed to be growing taller while he himself grew littler and littler. The blanket was smothering him, and the forest deer were closing in on him.

With a frightened bellow, he bolted through the circle of deer, going after Uncle Jim, trying to run to him. But the path rose and dipped, and the old mule seemed to be playing hide-and-seek. Half running, Brighty followed the hoof tracks. Occasionally a shaft of sunlight struck down on the mule and Brighty ran faster, his lungs pumping for air, his blanket flapping in the wind. Running made him cough, and he had to stop and wait for enough strength to go on. And so the distance between them widened and widened, until the white mule was nothing but a wisp of dust. Then even the dust was gone.

Burro-wise, Brighty stopped in his tracks. There was no use going on. He looked about him and saw cows huddled in a meadow, and a two-story ranch house squatting in a little cup of land. Tiredly, he turned in to join the cattle, who stood gazing in wide-eyed curiosity at him and his gaudy blanket.

The ranch house Brighty had come upon had been built by Mormon cowmen and was still used as summer headquarters. Homer Hobbs was helping the men there while he waited for Wiley's Camp to open. He had waved to Uncle Jim on his mule and was not surprised when Brighty showed up a little later.

Even with the blanket covering the burro from ears to tail, Homer recognized him and called to him softly by name. He led Brighty up to the house and coaxed him to drink warm cow's milk. But a lick of salt and a swallow of water were all he wanted.

With Homer's hands comforting him and straightening his blanket, Brighty fell into a kind of stupor and waited out the day. He was aware of calves bawling and cows answering. But these were faraway sounds, and the big-eared, brown-eyed faces were seen through a haze.

Late in the afternoon he started back to Uncle Jimmy's meadow, and arrived home only a few moments before he heard the galloping hoofbeats of the white mule.

Uncle Jim did not come to Brighty at once. He disappeared into the cabin just long enough to feed the squealing pup. Then out he came, arms loaded with a curious assortment — a bunch of carrots, a chunk of salt, and a washbasin filled with soapy water. The bottle of cough mixture he had carefully hidden in his back pocket.

"Now, Brighty," he smiled, "by all the laws of donkeydom ye should have a nacherel taste fer carrots. And I'm goin' to work on 'em right here so's to stir up yer saliva juices." He selected an extra large carrot and cut off the top with his knife. Then with a small auger he drilled a hole down the center. "By grab!" he chuckled as he worked. "If this idea was to click, I'd feel chesty as any doctor that had cured a croupy kid."

He pulled a funnel from his pocket and fitted it into the hole. Then he turned his back on Brighty and poured a little cough medicine into the carrot. Next he cut off the tip end, and using it as a cork, he carefully sealed the medicine inside.

All this while Brighty stood huddled in his blanket, watching. He saw Uncle Jim wash his hands furiously in the basin, wipe them on his pants, and take a whiff of them.

"Nary a trace o' medicine smell," he said. "Funny how I'll scrub and scour fer ye, boy, much as I dislike the shriveled-up feeling ye get from soap and water."

He picked up the carrot and held it to his nose, chuckling. "Smells nice and carroty!" Next he chiseled some salt off the salt block, pounded it fine with the butt of his knife, and sprinkled it over the carrot. "No one," he laughed, "not even a smart feller like ye, Brighty, would suspect that this-here goody is a capsoole with a nip o' cough-mix in it."

Brighty's head was nodding when Uncle Jim came over to him, the carrot outstretched on his hand. He stooped down, and for a long moment he held the carrot to Brighty's nose. Nothing happened. Just as he was about to give up in failure, he saw the nostrils flutter to draw in the smell. He saw the tongue slowly reach out to lick the salt. Then the lips closed on the carrot and his hand was empty. He heard the crunching sound and saw the jaws working, and the dark, sad eyes regard him.

A choking filled Uncle Jim's throat. "By thunder!" he said softly, "I don't know when I've been so tickled with myself! Presidents and burros ain't so different after all." He laughed in relief. "If

I recollect proper, I used to doctor up Teddy Roosevelt's dose in a cup o' hot tea!"

As the days went by, Brighty swallowed a hidden dose of medicine with every carrot he ate. And with each dose, his strength grew and his coughing petered out.

When he was all well again, he seemed so happy and frisky that Uncle Jim had to smile just looking at him. Mornings now, Brighty could hardly wait for the trip to the spring. Often he started out first, then came running back to hurry Uncle Jim along.

The summer spent itself with Brighty acting as waterboy for Uncle Jim and Homer Hobbs too. And he seemed more generous than ever in giving rides to the children at Wiley's Camp.

The sheriff came by every now and again to talk about mysterious doings at the Little Mimi Mine. He looked pounds thinner, and was irritable as a mule in a cloud of mosquitoes.

"It's my ulcers!" he fretted. "A crime unsolved is like a fire burnin' in the pit of my stomach. Every time I go into Old Timer's tunnel there's marks of fresh digging, but the digger himself ain't nowhere to be found!"

When autumn came, Brighty did not head toward the canyon. Each morning there he was, sitting white-bellied and happy in Uncle Jim's meadow.

"Hey, feller, ye're way late migratin'," Uncle Jim warned one day. "Why, I got on my long-handled drawers a'ready and an extry pair o' wool socks. Soon I'll be goin' over to Wiley's to take down the tents. And next thing ye know, I'll be tidyin' up my own cabin and lopin' off to Fredonia. It'd sure be funny were ye to hibernate in town with me!"

Less than a week later the sky promised a freeze, and Uncle Jim put a question to Brighty: "If'n ye ain't goin' to winter in the canyon where it's warm, how'd ye like to cozy up in the corral with my ole white mule tonight?"

He headed down the lane toward the corral, watching with pleasure as Brighty pranced along beside him. He lifted the gate poles, and Brighty started to go through the opening. But halfway in, he hesitated. He raised his head skyward, as if pondering some great decision. Then quite suddenly he backed out of the gate, his muzzle grazing Uncle Jim's shoulder. With a flirt of his heels, he bounded away toward his trail, a winking gray fleck in the dusk.

Uncle Jim put the poles back in place. He stood looking until he could see Brighty no more. Then he smiled his slow, understanding smile as he trudged back to the cabin alone.

Spider Web of Steel

DURING THE NEXT FEW YEARS, Brighty's trail from rim to river was pounded down by many feet — the split hoofs of mountain sheep and deer, the pads of cougar and coyote, the hoofs of horses and mules, and the booted feet of men.

Men felt the pull of the canyon, not in the way Brighty did — for its winter warmth and browse — but for its brooding mystery. More and more of them came, explorers and geologists and students of birds and butterflies and bees. And sometimes an artist set up his easel on a bulge of rock and painted, and tore up what he painted and began again.

Brighty, on his treks up and down, greeted these adventurers with hearty brays and often took potluck with them.

He spent several weeks with a bushy-haired artist, a giant of a fellow who was an excellent hand at baking. Brighty grew sleek and fat on johnnybread and hot biscuits and sugar cakes. In return, he did some light packing — an odd assortment of brushes, canvases, and tubes of paint. It was a pleasant arrangement for both. While the artist daubed his colors, using his hair as a brushwiper, Brighty was free to come and go.

What ended their friendship was a freak accident. One evening the man swung astride the burro to ride uptrail a way to their camping spot. He had never done this before. Everything might have gone along all right in spite of the weight of the man and the upward climb. Even the picture frame poking Brighty's ribs was not too painful, now that he had some fat on them. But a yellow jacket made a surprise landing on his rump and punched its stinger deep into his flesh.

"Ai—yee! Ai—yee! Ai—ai—ai!" Brighty yowled

in anguish. Up he went skewering into the air, while the unfortunate artist fell off backward, almost toppling into the canyon. As if this were not ill luck enough, his big boot smashed right through the newly done painting.

Even in his upside-down position, the artist broke into a rage. He jerked the picture off his foot, got up, and ran after Brighty, who was rubbing his hindquarters against a rock. He stood towering over the burro a moment. Then gripping the painting with both hands he lifted it high and brought it down — crash! — over Brighty's head. It stuck there at a crazy angle, like a clown's collar.

"You jackass!" he cried, picking up a rock. "Get out of my sight!"

Brighty needed no urging. The stinger was a poker of fire, driving him on up the rocky ledges.

It was hours later that a lone hiker, a little man with a butterfly net, came upon the burro sitting in the icy waters of the creek, crying in pain. The man put down his net, and when Brighty backed up to him showing no intent to kick, he examined the situation and soon removed the stinger. Then he lifted the picture over Brighty's head and studied what was left of it. He began to laugh. "Whoever painted this gaudy mess should've smashed it! But why," he wondered aloud, "why over the head of a poor little defenseless burro? —

"Say, I know who you are!" he exclaimed. "You're Bright Angel! You built this trail!" And he regarded the burro as if it stirred his pride to associate with so famous a character.

Once more Brighty's days were pleasant, although the butterfly man ate but two meals a day and they were puny compared to the artist's. As payment, he asked only small favors — the carrying of a few jars of formaldehyde, and sometimes a light bedroll.

But in time the man began to act as if he owned the burro. He wanted him at beck and call every waking moment. If Brighty so much as played in the creek or ambled off to browse, the man made a great to-do. Had he not rescued Brighty? That ungrateful wretch!

Some nights Brighty would purposely wander into a side canyon to be alone. And when morning came, he delighted in listening to the call of his name as it rang from cliff to cliff. Snorting to himself, he just rolled over and went right back to sleep.

Any delay in his butterfly hunt infuriated the man, so he made a bell out of a tin can and a pebble, and tied it around Brighty's neck. "Now," he said, clapping his small hands in triumph, "I'll be able to spot ex*act*ly where you are!"

But he had not reckoned with burro wiles. By practicing a little, Brighty learned to walk without the slightest nod of his head or the least sway of his body. Then the clapper in the bell hung silent! It turned into a regular game. The minute Brighty knew he was wanted, he tiptoed very slyly right behind the man, or went off and hid. When the need for him was past, he came trotting back, the bell tinkling merrily.

One morning, however, it was not to be free of the butterfly man that he sneaked off. It was a curiosity that pulled him. Deep in the inner gorge of his canyon there were strange thunderings. They belonged to neither wind nor river nor sky. They were sharper, louder than thunder, with long spaces of quiet between. Each time the rumble came, the very rock on which Brighty stood quaked. The tremors went running up and down his legs, and through his whole body. What could it be? It was frightening, and exciting too. Brighty had to know.

He turned tail on the little man, and once out of earshot, swung happily along, letting the bell tinkle as it would.

Down, down, down he went, stopping only to quiver and snort when the racket let loose. Once in the inner gorge he half ran to the river, and there he burst full upon the scene. It almost made his ears leap out of their sockets.

Across the four hundred feet of water, the opposite shore was alive with mules and men and tents and rigging of all kinds. And more mules, with great planks strapped to their sides, were footing their way down the face of the wall to the little hive of activity.

Brighty trumpeted his excitement. His eyes darted from mules to men and back again. Then all of a sudden a white cloud of smoke belched out of the black cliff above the scene. A terrifying explosion followed, with rocks bursting into air. Brighty felt the world shake beneath him. A steamy sweat broke out over his body. He ran for fear the smoke and rocks would leap the river. Heart pounding against his ribs, he hid under the green umbrella of a cottonwood tree. He stayed there a long time, until the roaring of the river told him the explosion was over.

Then cautiously he crept back to the river's edge. Nothing much had changed. Men were still moving about like ants busy on an anthill, and the mule train was still angling down the wall. As for the white smoke, it was gone, leaving in its place a gaping hole above a great spilling of rocks.

Fearful, yet fascinated, Brighty could not tear himself away. For two days more the explosions continued. When they finally ended, the busyness of the men increased. It even reached across the river and tapped Brighty on the shoulder.

What he saw on the third day was the cage swinging over the river toward him. When it reached his shore, a workman began unloading a wheelbarrow and big white bags. Done with his unloading, he wiped his sweating brow with his bare arm and looked around. Suddenly he spied the burro, and his face broke into a smile.

"Hey! You must be Brighty!" he yelled in a pleasant, booming voice. "Come here. You and me are going to build the bulkhead to hold the new bridge. That old cage'll soon be a goner."

In spite of Brighty's fear, curiosity was strong in him. He took a step forward, eyes and ears showing great interest.

The workman turned out to be a nice fellow — particular, too. He studied the texture of the sand down the river and up in the washes. "Too silty!" or "Too coarse!" he would say, testing it between his fingers. At last in a side canyon made by Phantom Creek he found some pockets of sand he liked.

"Just right!" he shouted.

He coaxed Brighty into packing load after load

of it. Then he mixed it with the cement from the white bags and built a bulkhead.

Meanwhile two big cables were pulled across the river. To Brighty they looked like the beginning of some huge spider's web. He watched by the hour. Watched brave men dangling in rope slings, anchor the cables high in the rock wall. Watched riggers work themselves along the cables, fastening hanger rods in place. Watched floor planks swung out, then eased onto the web. Watched big rolls of fencing unfurled and fastened to the side rails.

As the web grew, men scrambled over it and under it, and some seemed to be held in it like flies. Week on week the thing grew, and the steel of it shimmered in the sun and the wind tossed it as if it *were* a spider's web.

Late one afternoon Brighty was sitting on his haunches, his gaze on the swinging bridge and the men painting it. There was a look of yearning in his eye, as if he longed to cross the bridge to see what was on the other side. Green grass? Mesas to thunder across? Little long-eared creatures like himself?

The roar of the river shut out the lesser noises behind — hoofs sinking in the sand, men's voices, mules snorting. Not until the party was full upon him did Brighty start to his feet.

Brighty, B.A.

HE WHEELED, almost colliding with a white mule. And above the mule's face, looking between his ears, were the twinkling eyes of Uncle Jimmy Owen. Brighty's breath snortled. He pawed and pranced as the men on muleback laughingly rode herd on him until the whole little company was in among the cottonwoods, away from the roar of the river.

Uncle Jim swung a leg over his mule's head and slid out of his saddle. He went to Brighty and stood eye to eye with him. "Our whole canyon's changin', feller." His fingers worked gently in Brighty's mane. "Old Timer wouldn't like this new-fangled bridge. Traffic comin' and goin'. And folks pokin' and pryin' into his life."

He turned to a big-built man sitting a big horse. "Excuse me, Mr. Teddy," he said, "for harkin' to the past. Sure sign I'm gettin' old, ain't it?"

Theodore Roosevelt smiled, flashing wide-set teeth. "It's a natural feeling, Jim. We all buck change the way a mule bucks a strange load."

He dismounted, then glanced in Brighty's direction. "Isn't that the same fellow . . ." He broke off his sentence in the middle. "Of course it is! Brighty! You probably don't remember me. But I'll never forget the day that wild cougar leaped on your back."

Uncle Jim elbowed Brighty's neck, and Brighty's head gave a nod, as if he remembered too.

"Well, by George!" Mr. Roosevelt laughed. He turned to the other men who were gathering around. "Gentlemen," he said, "I'd like you to meet Bright Angel, the gamest burro in the world."

At Uncle Jim's signal, Brighty nodded all around

— to the government officials, to the engineers, and to the governor of Arizona too.

All the visitors bowed in mock dignity. They were feeling good after riding safely down the long trail. Now each took pride in tying his mule to a tree and pulling off the saddle without help from Uncle Jim.

Then they limbered up, stretching to relieve aching muscles. One by one they went off in different directions, as if the majesty of the canyon were a thing to worship alone.

When they came back, they found Uncle Jim making camp in the small spot shut in by the cottonwood trees. He had coffee simmering on a fire, and sticks sharpened for broiling lion steaks, and bread baking in a Dutch oven.

The night wind flowed down the canyon, and the men closed in around the fire while they ate their supper. Brighty joined them, his back against Uncle Jim, ready to accept any little handouts offered.

After their meal, Theodore Roosevelt polished his spectacles and settled himself in enjoyment of the blazing fire. "Gentlemen," he said, "I've come a long way to dedicate the new bridge. You have asked me to be the first to cross it."

He paused a moment, his eye looking back up the winding trail he had come. "But," he went on, "as I followed our guide down the twenty-one miles from the North Rim, I had time to do a little thinking."

The others nodded, as if their minds had been busy too.

Mr. Roosevelt leaned forward, his eyes pleased and eager. "If it meets with your approval," he said, "I should like to have Jim Owen, a true frontiersman, dedicate the new bridge and be first to cross it."

There was a little silence while the men looked at one another, then into the fire.

The governor of Arizona was first to speak. "If that is your wish, Mr. Roosevelt, I for one will be glad to honor it."

The other men agreed. One said, "Uncle Jimmy has bagged over three hundred mountain lions that were killing off the deer and threatening cattle and sheep. He's made the canyon safe for tourists. I would like to make a motion that Jim Owen be the first to walk across our newly finished bridge, and so to dedicate it to the peoples of the world."

"I second that motion," the governor said.

Theodore Roosevelt smiled at Uncle Jim. "Well?"

The old man loosened his neckerchief as if it

were choking him. Then he took off his hat and let the wind pick up what was left of his hair.

"Mr. Teddy," he faltered, "it ain't as if I didn't want to, but my back is up agin a li'l ole burro what *is* a frontiersman. Ask any old-timey canyon man. Ask trappers and miners and prospectors. Ask the Mormon sheepherders and cattlemen. They'll all tell ye, every last one o' them, it's Brighty here who's the real frontiersman. 'Twas his hoofs gouged out the trail which we all taken today. Ain't no engineer in the world could've built better!"

Brighty heard his name and wriggled closer, sighing and basking in the good feeling.

"Ye're all big wheels in this-here world," Uncle Jimmy smiled, looking around shyly, "an' me an' Brighty's just canyon fellers. But if'n ye don't mind, gentlemen, I'd like fer Brighty to be first to cross the bridge to the other side, where he ain't never been!"

Theodore Roosevelt stretched his legs and got up, grinning. To his delight, Brighty scrambled up too. They stood facing each other. "The bridge is intended for man and beast," he said. "Why couldn't *both* of these frontiersmen be first to cross — Uncle Jimmy Owen with Bright Angel at heel?"

There was a nodding of heads, as if each had thought up the idea on his own.

The next morning the sun lay bright along the rim, but it was still dark in the canyon when the sleeping camps on either side of the river stirred to life. Two fires began glowing, like eyes widespread. Brighty, on the north bank, was beside himself with happiness, running off to talk with the mules, then back to camp to smell the flapjacks browning and to nudge Uncle Jim to hurry and dish up.

Theodore Roosevelt was down on his knees, splashing his face with the clear water of Bright Angel Creek. The other men were trying to give Uncle Jim a hand with the cooking, and he was humoring them.

There was considerable talk for so early in the morning, and Brighty heard his name often. He heard it as he rolled in the sand, and he stopped rolling an instant, ears pricked. He heard it again as he munched his flapjacks, and his jaws stopped working to listen.

When breakfast dishes were done, Uncle Jim put his clean, reddened hands on Brighty's neck and faced around to the group. "Y'know, gentlemen," he said. "if ever was a big day fer a li'l ole burro, this here's it. I never been one to hamper wild critters with a lot o' trappin's, but seems like today he could be decked out some."

An idea struck the chief engineer. He took off the sun helmet he was wearing. "I won't be needing this," he said, "now the bridge is done." He spanned the distance between Brighty's ears with his hand, then took out his knife and cut two holes in the crown. "Here, Jim, you try it on him for size," he said when the holes were nice and round. "I've heard some jacks are tickly about their ears."

Uncle Jim shook his head. "I'll have to ask ye to please make them peepholes twicet as big, feller. The roots o' Brighty's ears is mighty stal'art."

While the engineer was working on his helmet, the geological-survey man began to sketch on a piece of blueprint paper. "That helmet," he chuckled, "needs a fitting emblem. I think wings to represent Bright Angel would be just the ticket." And with a few quick cuts he produced a shapely pair.

Word somehow flew to the camp across the river that Brighty was to take part in the dedication ceremonies, and a few men came over ahead of time. Danny the cook was one of them. He brought a pocketful of bright-colored tapes. "These came from around the hams," he said. "How about braiding 'em into Brighty's mane and tail?"

The men were like boys, each trying to outdo the others. The chief packer made a flour-water paste to stick the wings onto the helmet. "Paste 'em up high enough," he said, "and I'll paint 'B.A.' under the wings with the left-over bridge paint."

The surveyor broke out in laughter. "My brother just graduated from college. He's got ears almost as big as Brighty's, and he signs his name with a 'B.A.' after it. Wait'll I tell him about this!"

Uncle Jim turned to the man. "What's it stand for?"

"It means 'Bachelor of Arts.' "

"I'll be danged," Uncle Jim smiled as he combed Brighty's mane with his fingers, "if that don't fit Brighty too. He's a bachelor all right, at least as fur as I know."

Brighty yawned and stretched his body in a luxurious curve. He let the men crowd around as Uncle Jimmy braided the red and blue tapes into the stubbly mane.

There were no hobbles or pickets to hold him, no restraints whatever. And so he stayed in their midst, feeling happy and wanted.

A Gift for Uncle Jim

BESIDE THE COTTONWOOD TREES a little spit of sand lay as level as if it had been graded for the occasion. All the crew were assembling—workmen in clean shirts, Indians bare to their waists, and boss-men in trim khaki.

"Everybody looks so slicked up and solemn," one said, "makes you feel like you're at a wedding or a funeral."

Facing the crew were the government men, headed by Theodore Roosevelt. And a little apart from them, like actors backstage, stood Uncle Jimmy Owen and Brighty.

"It wouldn't take no more'n a fleabite," Uncle Jim whispered into Brighty's ear, "to make me bolt into the blue yonder."

Just then a voice boomed out. It belonged to the governor of Arizona, and he began like a roll call. "Mr. Roosevelt, members of the Park Board, engineers of this great bridge, and workmen all."

He paused, waiting for his echoes to catch up with him. But even when they had smalled down to nothing, he stood quiet, as if the occasion had suddenly grown too big for him.

"This is a wedding, gentlemen," he said at last. "A wedding between the North Rim and the South. Until now the Colorado River has been a mighty cleaver chopping at the land of Arizona, separating the north from the south."

The governor warmed to his subject. "Think on it, gentlemen! Here the river is but four hundred feet across. Yet its treachery has forced men to travel more than two hundred miles around to get from one rim to the other.

"A few dared swim across it, but we know not

how many were sucked down into the river that never gives up its dead."

Uncle Jim's hand reached out to stroke Brighty, his mind on Old Timer.

"Early in this century," the governor went on, "the Mormons of northern Arizona grew tired of making a wide circuit to go just a few miles. They wanted to travel beeline. So one day an enterprising fellow flew a kite across to a man on the opposite bank. And the man waiting had a heavy string ready to tie onto the kite. From this simple spanning, the first cable was strung."

Heads bobbed, remembering the story.

"Back in those days," the governor went on, "men never dreamed that materials for a bridge could be packed down the perpendicular walls of the canyon. They tried to make the best of a bad situation. First they swung themselves across the cable in an old boatswain's chair, and later the chair was replaced by a cage. But even so," and here the governor shook his head sadly, "the strain of pulling and braking caused the strongest of men to fall down in exhaustion when they reached the opposite bank."

Heads nodded again, and Uncle Jim forgot his nervousness, his mind living the past.

"It was in the little wooden cage," the governor's

voice mounted, "that Theodore Roosevelt once crossed the river. Yet the hardships he suffered did not lessen his appreciation of the canyon. It was he, as President, who proclaimed it a National Monument."

Brighty threw back his head and let out a mighty bray.

No one laughed. It was more like an amen than a jeer.

"It is therefore with great pride that we call upon Theodore Roosevelt to dedicate this marvel of engineering, this great new suspension bridge."

The governor's last words were drowned out by the clamor of applause and shouting. Here was no place for city hand clapping. Here was a time and place for roaring like the river itself.

Theodore Roosevelt's smile flashed big. He too felt high-spirited. He groped in his mind for the right words. There was a waiting look in every eye, and ears straining to hear.

"Soldiers of peace," he boomed out at last, "you have fought a hard campaign against a mighty opponent. That you have won is evidence not only of a great skill but of a great faith. You have spanned a barrier between these mile-high walls — a barrier that has been a sinister, death-dealing force. For centuries the Colorado River has dared men, defied men, defeated men, drowned men. Day and night it has roared its challenge. You accepted that challenge — a hundred men working as one, a hundred pairs of hands and feet and lungs, a hundred minds and hearts working as one. This spider web of steel is everlasting proof of the power of working together."

Uncle Jim was absently fiddling with Brighty's ears. He wished almost that he knew how to slow time or stop it altogether, so that he and Brighty could always be at a little distance from big doings, just hearing and seeing. He listened, and liked the dignity of the next words.

"Of what value are dreams and blueprints," Mr. Roosevelt asked, "if all of you — architects, engineers, packers, and workmen — have not found a power and glory in working together?"

"None!" chorused the crowd.

High up on a cliff, a ragged, black-bearded creature, more animal than man, peered down on the proceedings. Brighty's ears shot forward. Only he saw the figure before it slid from view.

"But as with any great accomplishment," Mr. Roosevelt went on, "there comes a feeling of sadness when it is done. I've seen strong men cry when a job's finished, as if the doing were more fun than the getting through."

The men nodded in silent agreement, surprised that an outsider could understand so well.

"For us, however, this is a day of rejoicing, when two lands rent asunder are once more joined together."

Brighty chose this very moment to bray his brassiest, and now the men laughed with him until the whole canyon burst into a joyful noise.

Theodore Roosevelt's laughter was last to quiet down. He had to wipe his glasses and then his eyes before he could talk.

"Brighty," he said, "who is supposed to be awaiting his cue backstage, reminds me to get on with the business at hand. Gentlemen, I came here to accept the distinguished honor of being first to cross your bridge. But now I am here, I forego that honor."

A great silence came over the gathering.

"I forego it in favor of James Owen — cowboy, lion-killer, frontiersman."

Mr. Roosevelt cleared his throat, and his manner became confidential. He looked from one face to another, enjoying himself to the full. "One time on a lion hunt," he said, "I caught Jim fondling my rifle with his eye. It put me in mind of a lad hankering for his first pair of cowboy boots. Right then I decided that someday he should own a rifle exactly like mine. So I've packed it all the way down here, little thinking to make a speech about it. But if you do not mind . . ."

He let his sentence dangle in mid-air while he walked a few paces away to a boulder. He reached behind it for the rifle and carefully removed the leather casing. Then he came back to his audience, turning the rifle so that the gold plate on the stock was face up. Adjusting his eyeglasses, he read aloud the simple inscription:

TO JAMES OWEN
FROM HIS FRIEND
THEODORE ROOSEVELT

For a few moments not a voice was lifted nor a hand clapped, as with uncertain step Uncle Jim went forward, holding out trembling hands to accept the rifle.

And still the men were silent. But when Uncle Jim tried to read the words through a blur of tears, it was then the tide of happiness burst.

Well Done!

CLUTCHING THE RIFLE TO HIM, Uncle Jim smiled through misted eyes. A few words started in him, but they died on his lips. He turned and went quickly to Brighty and brought him to face the group. With one hand on the burro's shoulder and the other holding his rifle, he looked to Mr. Roosevelt to get on with the doings.

The men grinned at Brighty's helmet and ribbons. One nudged his neighbor and pointed. "Little old low-life's in high company today," he said.

The color mounted in Uncle Jim's face. Suddenly he wanted the chance to speak.

Mr. Roosevelt understood and nodded.

"'Low-life' is it!" Uncle Jim exploded. "Who was it Jesus chose to carry him into Jerusalem? Who?"

The question hung quivering in the air. Jim Owen took a step forward. "Why, 'twas a li'l long-eared feller, the spit image o' Brighty. And on all sides folks gathered round, and some ran on ahead, layin' down a carpet o' palm leaves. Why, I kin just see the li'l feller pickin' his way like he knowed he was workin' fer God."

The men's eyes twinkled.

"And mind ye, fellers!" Uncle Jim shook his big-knuckled forefinger. "Every since that day, burros has been marked with the cross. Look-a-here." He traced the black stripe down Brighty's back and the crossbar over his shoulder. "See them lines? Where'd ye find a stouter-marked cross than this 'un?"

Now the anger washed out of Uncle Jim, and he looked around helplessly, embarrassed that he had talked so much.

Mr. Roosevelt picked up the thought and spliced onto it. "Yes, gentlemen, Brighty has earned the emblem he wears. He had borne burdens and blazed trails. He has packed the sand and cement that built the very bulwark of the bridge. What could be more fitting than that these two frontiersmen, James Owen and Bright Angel, dedicate the new bridge?"

Voices went up in cheers, and relief too, as the men realized that the solemn speechmaking was over. The cook stepped out, dried his lips on his sleeve, and lifted a trumpet.

"What will it be, Danny?" Mr. Roosevelt asked.

The cook unpursed his lips. "I'm going to play the extry favorite the men wanted when things was tough. It's 'Onward, Christian Soldiers,' sir!"

The stirring music rolled forth, and to its rhythm Uncle Jim and Brighty marched out of the cottonwood shelter toward the great new bridge. The audience followed like a platoon of soldiers.

The sun struck down on the river and the wind swayed the bridge, causing a black shadow to waver across the water. Now the whole company of men stood at attention. It was as if the months of lifting and pounding and sweating had worked into this moment.

Even with the river drowning the music, the pulsating beat went on. Uncle Jim stepped to it, stepped around now to the apron leading onto the bridge.

Brighty, who had been marching beside him, stopped dead still. In a flash of remembering, did he see the cage in place of the bridge? Did he see his jailer atop the cage, and himself hanging by the neck? No one knows what went on in his mind, but all at once he grew rigid.

A tenseness came over the crowd too. What if Brighty balked? What if he refused to cross, and so spoiled the ceremony? The cook blew with all his lung power, trying to give Brighty courage, and the men nearest him made a wall of their bodies, closing off escape.

One cupped his hands to his mouth. "Maybe his stubborn is up!" he yelled, reaching for a willow whip.

Uncle Jim stopped him with a look. Then he turned his back on the man and faced the swaying bridge. Gingerly he thrust out his foot, easing his weight onto the apron. When it gave a little to his step, he stood quiet a long moment, trying to show Brighty how solid it was in spite of the give.

Then without moving his feet, he twisted his body, bent down, and ran his hand along Brighty's leg as if he had nothing in mind but to examine the scars. Slowly, carefully, he lifted the tiny hoof and placed it on the bridge alongside his own.

This was the crucial second. One false move,

and Brighty would spin and bolt through the wall of men.

Scarcely breathing, Uncle Jim pretended to examine the other foreleg. Then slowly he brought it, too, onto the bridge. And with Danny blowing his lungs out, and the men straining forward, shouting the words

> Onward, Christian soldiers!
> Marching as to war,
> With the cross of Jesus
> Going on before!

Brighty and Uncle Jim started moving, started teetering across that great long span. One foot forward and then another. They were letting the bridge sway sideways with the wind as it was meant to, and up and down with the weight of their bodies.

Now they were halfway across! On and on they went, step by step, like proud soldiers on the homeward stretch. Then at last they touched the apron on the other side. The roar of voices drowned the river as Uncle Jim lifted the helmet from Brighty's head and gave him a friendly slap of "Well done."

Battle on the Mesa

BRIGHTY STOOD QUIVERING, with the river streaming by behind him and the men on the opposite shore starting to cross. He could feel Uncle Jim's hands undoing his braids, and he let the hands work as he might let a butterfly light on him. It was as if Uncle Jim belonged to faraway times and places, while he, Brighty, faced the wonder of a whole new world.

His eyes traveled eagerly up and up the south wall, and his ears were pokers into the future. He swung them to and fro, and he had a rapt look, as though listening to a melody half remembered. This south wall of the canyon seemed like, yet strangely unlike, the north. And while his eyes climbed, three wild burros suddenly ran out on a little mesa above and stood staring his way. Glancing up, Uncle Jim caught sight of them, and he too gazed fascinated. Their ears showed stiff and erect over the brink of the mesa, and for a long time the three stood frozen. Then the creature in the middle rose up on his hind legs, like a boxer ready to fight.

Brighty pulled in a breath. His body began to shake.

Uncle Jim chuckled. He brought his hands down on the burro's back, half a pat, half a shove. "Go ahead, boy. Might do ye good to mix with yer own folks; it's only right and nacherel."

With a snort of ecstasy, Brighty leaped forward and started racing up the wall. He was terrified that the creatures might not wait for him. He bounded from crag to crag, trembling with excitement. When at last he clattered up over the lip of the mesa, he saw that the three jacks were not alone. Dark-eyed jennies and colts were huddled in little bunches behind them. But it was the big black, snorty fellow in the center that held Brighty transfixed. He was hypnotized by the fire and frenzy of the jack.

He slowed, approaching cautiously.

At once the black drove the two small jacks into the bunch. Then, with a bellowing whistle, he came charging the intruder, yellow teeth bared, sides going in and out, forefeet raking the air.

In joyous rage, Brighty met him head on. It was a fight, the big battle-scarred veteran against the gray rookie. Like men in a ring they sparred — dancing, punching, interlocking, breaking apart. Behind the fighters the eyes of the mares gleamed darkly. They saw hoofs strike home at ribs, at chests; saw jaws rip pieces of hide; saw drops of blood stain the sand.

Screams echoed down the canyon, followed by rasping grunts. Then the dull sound of bodies meeting again and again.

The black's breath rattled in his nose. He meant to kill the gray stranger, to fasten his teeth on the throat, to puncture the big vein. He fought with cunning, biting at Brighty's legs to get him down, then going for his neck. Twice Brighty's knees buckled, and the black tried to seize the vein. But Brighty wrenched free, only to take a fresh battering of hoofs.

Again he went down. This time he pulled the black with him, and for a few seconds sucked in the air his lungs craved. Each breath was a quick surge of power, and now he was up again. But the black lunged at him, pushed him toward the edge of the mesa. For an instant, Brighty caught the red warning of the abyss. He slued around, using his forefeet as ramrods, kicking out in wild fury, giving his foe punch after punch in the ribs. With a groan the black fell heavily on his side, the wind knocked out of him.

Only a moment Brighty stood over him. Then the defeated jack picked himself up and limped off. And suddenly Brighty heard his own voice sounding the triumphant bray of the victor.

The jennies and colts stirred apart, some answering in sniffles and some in high whinnies. Brighty did a quick leap skyward. Instinctively he knew that now he was their leader.

A New World for Brighty

THE WORLD SUDDENLY OPENED OUT for Brighty. It was a new kind of freedom, a freedom charged with power and strength. He was king, and his realm big beyond belief. The Tonto Plateau hung like an enormous shelf on the south wall of the canyon. It spread flat and green, so different from the canyon he had known. He could look out upon acres and acres of sagebrush and cactus, and then up at the pyramids that rose like a throne at his back.

Brighty had never set foot on a mesa before. The immensity of it gave him a wild-spirit feeling. He raced his band of mares and colts across it, and for sheer fun he skirted them dangerously along the edges where the walls fell off vertically into black space.

Every deep-drawn breath was exciting. Instead of one trail, there were hundreds of tiny corkscrew trails worn by the feet of many burros. Years ago they had been turned loose by miners and trappers, and now lived in wild bands. But so vast was the mesa, there was room for all.

Brighty traveled like a king on the land. He explored the labyrinth of trails. Some, he found, crissed and crossed, ending up nowhere at all, but others led to fine watering places. Here he took on the full stature of ruler.

As he and his flock approached a spring, he tasted the wind, sampling it for the scent of enemies. Had some rival jack preceded? Was he hiding in ambush, ready to steal Brighty's newfound family?

At the first scent of a foe, Brighty wheeled his band in the opposite direction, sometimes nipping the mares and kicking at the foals to force them to safety. He brooked no foolishness. He knew that suffering thirst was better than fighting to the death.

But often as not the breeze blew fresh. Then they all ran snorting to the water, drinking their fill and afterward rolling in the mud around it.

Brighty was an intelligent, devoted father, and he and his family lived in a little paradise of their own, a world of sun and plenty in the heart of the canyon. Sometimes days passed without their sighting another living creature.

But even when their world seemed snug and secure, Brighty's eyes forever searched the distance, picking out movement miles away—an eagle coasting down the sky, a coyote or wolf mounting a rock to look for prey.

Early in his career as leader, Brighty developed his own signals. A rumbling snort meant, "All's well." But a shrill cry said, "Danger, mares! Bunch up! Gather in your colts!"

The jennies obeyed in a flash. At the first alarm they flew around in a whirling vortex, herding their colts into dead center. Meanwhile Brighty turned on the wolf or coyote, driving him off with savage ferocity.

There were man enemies, too. Indians crept soundlessly on moccasined feet, trying to steal the burros. They were smarter than wolves, coming always when the wind blew their scent away. But

Brighty lost only a few foals to them, for his eyes were sharp, and the mares and colts could outrun the fleetest Indian.

Gradually his youthful gaiety gave way to sharp watchfulness. A new Brighty he was, able to size up an opponent, sensing instantly whether to fight or flee, or merely to stand defiant.

Outwardly, too, he changed. He became thinner, shaggier, and the hair over his eyes bushed out, giving him a wild, fierce look. When the wind ruffled his coat, it revealed the scars of many battles.

The days came and went, winter and summer, cold and heat. For three long years Brighty stayed with his flock. The urge to migrate was stilled. He seemed to forget the world of men — the lion smell of Uncle Jim, the beaver smell of Jake Irons, the sugar-candy sweetness of Homer and the children at Wiley's Camp. There was room in his mind for only his mares and the little foals he had fathered.

And then, in the middle of a sunlit morning, Brighty's new world came crashing down. He had closed his eyelids to snatch a moment's sleep. It was a windless day, with the sun warm to his back. His family was within easy calling distance, and he dozed standing, while the soft sounds of the colts suckling and the mares grinding the sagebrush lulled him deeper to sleep.

At first there was only a far-off speck on the wall above, a speck as still as a winter fly. Then slowly it began crawling down the wall, and as it crawled it quickened pace.

Brighty woke to sigh and to shift his weight. He took time to scan the cliffs above, but just as he did, the oncoming figure passed from sight around a turn. Grunting in contentment, he closed his eyes again, feeling safe for the moment and lazy.

So still was the wind and so deep his sleep that he neither smelled nor heard the swift-footed thief approaching. Then all at once his blood curdled to a ringing scream.

Instantly he was sharp awake. A glance told him that here was a foe he had fought before, a young Palomino jack easily defeated.

Brighty filled his lungs and let out a bugle cry that sent his mares into a huddle. Then, with ears laced back, he rushed at the young stallion.

The air, so peaceful a moment ago, suddenly became a sandstorm with dust rising, and little stones spitting, and hoofs lashing out like forked lightning.

Within the sand cloud, Brighty's breath hurt in his lungs. His nostrils smarted, and his eyes burned and watered. He blinked furiously, trying to see which way the hammer blows were coming. But the sand blinded him, and he seemed never to duck in time. The young jack caught him blow upon blow, then raked and ripped him with savage teeth. Brighty flailed wildly and missed.

And then, in the very heat of the fight, he deliberately slowed his hoofs. It was as if he suddenly realized the young jack had grown in bulk and weight, while he himself had faded. He knew it was impossible to win; it could only be a fight to the death.

Struggling free of the battering hoofs, he burst out of the sand cloud, running desperately toward the river. Two jennies started after him, but the Palomino drove them back into the bunch as the shrill bray of the conqueror sent cold shivers down Brighty's spine. With never a backward glance, he stumbled his lonely way. His shoulders were streaked with blood, his whole body ached, and defeat hung heavy upon him.

A Voice from the Past

BRIGHTY STAGGERED DIZZILY across the mesa. He could breathe now without swallowing grains of sand, but the freshness seemed gone from the air.

A chain of hoofprints showed him the way ahead, hoofprints made by his own feet and his mares, and lighter tracks made by the little fellows. As he stopped to snuff them, he felt a homelessness he had never known before. With downcast eyes he followed the chain along until it veered sharply away in a return circle. There, at the lip of the mesa, he halted and stared bleakly downward to the yellow river and the threadlike bridge across it.

A small wind rose. It blew cool against the welts on his body and on his neck where a patch of skin was torn. For a long time he stood looking outward into space, a woebegone figure, swaying over the brink. He seemed to be waiting — waiting perhaps for some one of his jennies or colts to see him off. But no one came. Only the wind blowing restless, and a hawk wheeling in an endless circle. He shivered and pressed his eyelids tight together, struggling to stay on his feet.

When the dizziness was over, he started down the steep wall. Once he had bounded up this very cliff in sharp ecstasy. Now, slowly, he let himself down, step by step, ears drooping, tail tucked in.

It was shadowy night when at last he reached the river. Ring-tailed cats made a glow with their eyes as they danced around, facing up at him. The moon was rising big over the rim, and it shone full on Brighty, on his dark, sad eyes and the cross on his back. He looked up at the moon, and it was as if he had held back too long. He let his head fall forward, and from deep in his throat came the dry sobbing of a soul wrenched by loneliness.

But no one heard. The moon only climbed higher, and the river roared its way to the sea.

Sun on the river, moon on the river, wind and rain on the river. Brighty detested the mad, muddy thing. Day on day he ran wildly along the shore. He seemed now to remember the other side, and it called to him as home. He longed to leap the river, to find Bright Angel Creek, to wade and wallow in it; then to climb the long trail to Uncle Jim and the green mountain meadow.

If only some hand would help him cross the bridge again! And while he ran frantic one day, a voice shouted above the river, "Nice Brighty!"

He spun around to see a shaggy-haired man with pin eyes squinting and gold teeth grinning. The man stood only a dozen feet away, his pots and pans and a string of pelts on the ground beside him.

"Nice Brighty! Nice Brighty!" he kept repeating. Suddenly the man began digging a hole in the sand. Then moving swiftly he gathered dead grass and twigs and laid a fire in it. With one eye on the burro, he took a jar of sour dough from his pack and began making biscuits.

Brighty sat down at a safe distance away. He recognized the voice and smell of Jake Irons, even with the added years and change of clothes. He followed every move of the familiar man actions, and his nostrils gathered in the pleasant smell of burning mesquite. He felt a little less forlorn; he even dozed a bit, waiting for the biscuits to bake. When he awoke, they were done and cooling in the wind.

Cautiously he footed his way toward them, watching as the man's hand broke one off and held it outstretched. At the instant when Brighty's jaws clamped down on it, the man's other hand came sneaking from behind his back. With a quick movement, he coiled a rope around Brighty's neck.

The bearded face was a smirk of triumph, and the rusty voice croaked, "Who said lightning don't strike twice! Eh, broomtail?"

With a laugh, Jake Irons tied a second rope to Brighty's collar. Knotting the free end, he wedged it between two boulders. Now that the burro was fast, his hands were free. He scooped up a few pebbles into an old tomato can and pressed the lid in place then tied one end of a cord around the can.

"How'd you like this against your rump?" he asked, spinning the tin can and letting it thwack against a rock. Brighty shied in panic. He jerked up until the halter rope snapped him back.

Now Irons came toward him, his grease-stained mackinaw almost touching the burro's nose. "That Old Timer of yours!" he shouted. "He was a bigger jackass than you. What good's a rich vein if you can't sell the ore! Do y'ever see a miner here get rich? No! They dig and they dig, and they die!"

He crouched down over Brighty, working himself into a fury. "It'd take a thousand jacks a thousand years to pack the stuff out. Listen, low-life!" He grabbed a firmer hold on the lead rope and pulled Brighty's head up. "Where do you think I been all these years? I been diggin' and doin' and hidin' until my belly's sick.

"And you know what you're going to do about it?" His hand spun the tin can in a threat. "You're going to lead me to Utah, that's what! Old Timer said you know the way up to the North Rim. I'll hit a new state and find a new way of thievin'."

Brighty made no movement or cry. The rattling tin can filled him with dread. He let the man swing a pack over his back and the pelts across the pack.

Now Irons released the halter rope from the boulders and pulled it over his own shoulder, drawing up the slack. He leaned forward and tried moving toward the bridge, fully expecting Brighty to balk. To his surprise, the burro stepped on his heels, almost sending him sprawling.

Brighty was going *his* way!

At the apron to the bridge, however, the burro came to a firm halt. He waited to have one foreleg lifted up, then the other, remembering how he had crossed before.

Instead, Irons whiplashed the tin can against his

hips. With a cry of terror, Brighty leaped onto the bridge. The sudden weight rocked it up and down, and the wind tossed it until his stomach churned with the double motion. He tried to plant his feet, but again the tin can crashed against his hindquarters and shot him forward.

He staggered along the plank floor, trying to balance, but his legs were boneless as rags. He felt his shoulders striking the wire fencing — first one shoulder, then the other — and his knees buckling, and the rope jerking him up. He tottered forward, reeling, slipping, crumpling, straightening, then staggering onward again, while the man laughed crazily and jumped up and down to make the bridge sway the more.

Sweat oozed out of Brighty's skin, and the river roared in his ears. And just when he could stand the noise and the seasickness no longer, he felt a mighty poke which landed him on the solid footing of the other shore.

For a long moment he stood there, his sides heaving and the air going into him. The man stood too, using his sleeve to wipe the sweat glistening on his forehead. Then his eyes moved greedily upward, ledge on ledge, precipice on precipice, to the rimtop, to the sky beyond. "Utah! Utah!" he shouted. "Across the line I'll be safe!"

On to Utah!

BRIGHTY FELT A PULSING OF STRENGTH. His legs began to hold him without trembling. And all at once he gave a snort of glee. He had crossed the river! This was his world, his *own* world — the solid little delta on which he stood, and Bright Angel Creek chattering up at him.

He tore loose from Jake Irons and, braying in joy, ran to the creek. He let it wash his feet and foam and bubble around his knees. He kicked and sudsed it onto his belly. His pack was no weight at all. Home! The beautiful creek, his! The whole north wall, his! The meadow waiting, his!

Eagerly, as if to make up for lost time, he began racing upward. He was unmindful of the man's desperate attempt to follow. "How long it has been!"

Brighty's happiness seemed to say. Even the gravel and shale of the path were friendly to his feet. The willow branches had not forgotten him either; they scratched his back and roughed his ears.

Again and again he crossed the creek, sometimes ducking his muzzle to let the water flow cool between his bridle teeth; and sometimes he just stood looking around, splay-legged as any colt. Once, far behind, he caught a glimpse of Jake Irons wading across the creek, holding his shoes on high.

Whenever Brighty stopped for a breather, he flattened himself against a bush of silver sage or a grayed rock. Irons meanwhile, afraid the burro had made off with his pack, came running and puffing to find him. Often he stopped to mop his brow quite near the hiding place. Then Brighty would dart ahead, heehawing in laughter.

Another mile of trail and another, and now when Brighty looked back, he saw the man face down in the creek, half sobbing with thirst and exhaustion. He swiveled his ear. That sound! It was the nearest thing to a bray he had heard since leaving the mesa. He answered it full steam. But the man did not reply. He had drunk too freely of the icy water and was bent double with cramps.

It was no fun playing hide-and-seek alone, so Brighty took a short nap. When he awoke, Jake

Irons was up and hovering over a fire in a half-tunnel of rock nearby. Brighty sniffed the air. Fire meant food and perhaps riddance of his pack. He edged toward it.

"You beast! You broomtail!" the man shouted, remembering the tricks played on him. "If I didn't need you for a guide, I'd — I'd slit your throat and leave your body to the ravens." He broke off his shouting to remove Brighty's pack.

A cold wind blew over the shoulder of rock. It made a plaintive sound as it spiraled down Brighty's ears. He turned tail and drew closer to the fire.

"Low on grub," Irons muttered darkly, "and me having to waste half on a burro!"

Somewhere a coyote howled, and the canyon answered him.

Brighty stood waiting for his food, and as he waited, a speck of snow fell on his nose. A few flakes touched the fire, made little hisses, and were gone. But away from the fire, on bushes and junipers, they hung like tiny white stars. Brighty walked to the very edge of the cliff and thrust his head out into space. He caught a few flakes and tasted them on his tongue — something new and delicious!

In silence the burro and the man ate their meager

lunch. The wind rose and a whirl of snow swooped into the shelter, powdering the man haunched over his coffee. He leaped to his feet in panic. He had never climbed the north wall before. In a snowstorm he would need the burro more than ever.

"I dreamt this blizzard last night!" he called out in alarm. "I dreamt the law was after me. They trailed my footprints. I got to go on!"

Quickly he shook the blanket free of snow, wrapped his skillet and coffeepot and the beaver pelts inside, stuffed cold biscuits in his pocket. He threw the pack on Brighty and jerked the ropes around his belly.

Then he turned to pick up the tin can with the pebbles, but there was no need to use it. Brighty was already out of reach. He had set the compass in his mind for the North Rim. Up ahead in the snow clouds there would be another kind of man, a gentle man, waiting to welcome him.

He bent his head to the climb, and at first the snow was pleasant to his face and he went with steady stride. But as they climbed higher, a wild mass of white billowed into the canyon. It closed in on the figures toiling up the wall and muffled all sound until the dead stillness threw terror into the man. He cried out, and the words he cried were, "Bright Angel! Bright Angel!"

Brighty had no ears for the rasping voice. He was completely baffled by his first snow. One moment it was a frosted star to taste on the tongue, the next a whipsnap of lightning trying to blind him.

Gruntingly, he defied the stinging lashes. He groped with his feet and used the pack as a feeler, scraping it along the walls. He gained a dozen yards and stopped to catch his breath, and another dozen yards while the snow sifted down into his ears and through his coat to the skin.

On turns of the trail, his head took the full fury of the storm. But his feet were sure, testing the slippery rocks for toeholds and, inch by inch, ledge by ledge, moving him on.

At a stopping place, Jake Irons caught up and clutched Brighty's ropelike tail to pull himself along. Before, it had been the man's desperate urge to top out. Now it was the burro's. He moved steadily upward, letting his tail be a towrope, letting it pull the man as if he were a dead thing — a sled or a log. Hoofprints and footprints were interlocking now, and relentlessly the wind and the snow were erasing them both.

The way steepened into rocky steps, and Brighty knew that he had come to the Devil's Backyard. The storm had muffled the noise of Ribbon Falls and Roaring Springs. He had gone right by without hearing their din. He stumbled on a tree root and almost fell to the rocks below, but the tree itself caught him.

Again the man cried out, "Bright Angel! Bright Angel!" But only the wind replied.

The sky darkened with fast-moving clouds, and the wind spiraled upward into the clouds. It sucked out more snow and blew it over the rocks until they had no shape at all. It buried the trail too, as if it had never been.

And still Brighty trudged on in his own peculiar way, sometimes almost crawling on his knees, sometimes taking the steps at a leap.

The man groaned, "Whoa! I can't breathe!"

But Brighty was a creature homing, a creature who must go on in spite of ice and snow. He could no longer see the way in front of him, but the pattern was fixed in his mind. The snowflakes melted on his eyelashes and stung hotly when he blinked, then froze into tiny icicles. Ice formed too on the feathers of his legs and cut his pasterns as he walked.

And still he kept on, slipping, struggling, feet and muscles aching, lungs burning. When he stopped to blow, he heard the hollow voice crying, "Food! Food! I'm starving!"

He glanced behind and saw Irons huddled into

his coat, gnawing on a frozen biscuit. Deliberately he ran away from the man.

In panic at being left alone, Irons dropped his biscuit, scrambled after Brighty, groped for the tail, caught it, pulled himself up. And now hoofprints and footprints interlocking again, and the two creatures all shrouded in snow.

As Brighty climbed onward, he was aware that the trail had begun to widen out. He no longer needed to hug the wall. There were trees on both sides now, and the slope was gentler. The struggle was almost over.

With Irons hanging on, he jog-trotted the homestretch. And when at last he topped the rim, he seemed to rout the storm. The snow thinned, ending abruptly, and a soft mist rolled in over the forest. Suddenly a burst of sun pierced the mist and flung a rainbow, like a triumphant arch of victory, across the sky.

A delicious home feeling welled up in Brighty. He wanted to run, to bray. In spite of his weariness, he was conscious of an old remembered joy. He saw ahead the trees that Uncle Jimmy had marked with a notch and a slit. He, Brighty, had packed the hatchet to mark these very trees! He had completed the journey.

This spot of earth was Home.

The Deserted Cabin

THROUGH AISLES OF ASPEN AND PINE, Brighty headed for Uncle Jim's cabin. He ignored the man's pull on his tail and the whining cry behind. His small hoofs, caked with ice, shuffled in and out of the snow with rhythmic strength. He could feel rope burns on his sides where the straps had rubbed, and his pack had grown very heavy, but there was happy purpose in his step.

Confidently he entered the lane winding down into the meadow. But now as his eyes saw it, he stopped dead. A chill of fear swept over him. The meadow was a glaze of white, a sealed-in land, all emptiness. There was no sign of life anywhere. No creature stirred, no man nor mule nor hound. Not even a bird. Everything had changed. Where green grass had been, there was instead this smooth crystal sea. And the cabin was most changed of all. It looked littler, and it crouched down in the corner of the meadow like some white-haired crone with window-glass eyes.

Brighty stood helpless in the quiet world of white. Except for the black smudges of his eyes he was snow-frosted too, like the meadow and the trees and the little cabin.

The rainbow had faded, and the low sun threw only the palest of shadows across the snow. Slowly Brighty shuffled toward the cabin. He stopped in front of the porch and sounded a long-drawn bray. His ears tipped forward, listening. But there was no answering sound. All he heard was his heart beating, and all he saw was a spume of snow churning in a little gust of wind.

The cabin door remained closed.

As the silence continued, Irons came alive. He let go Brighty's tail and glanced up at the cabin chimney to make sure the gray wisp above it was cloud, not smoke. Then he stamped onto the porch and knocked loudly on the door. He waited a moment, his breath making a hoarse whisper in the stillness. Then turning sideways, he threw his body against the door. It flew open so easily he fell sprawling on his face.

Brighty stepped in over him and halted in bewilderment. The place seemed colder than the out-of-doors. A hat and a jacket hung on a wall, but the smells they gave off were old and faint. He brayed to bring the place alive, but all it did was to stir Jake Irons.

The man sat up, rubbing his shins while he stared intently around the room as if his eyes might be playing tricks. He picked himself up and pushed at the walls to make sure they were real. When they did not budge, he closed the door behind him and gave Brighty a jolt with his knee. "Not bad, jughead," he laughed harshly. "Not half bad!"

Still remembering his dream, he shoved a trunk-sized box against the door and then looked about. He noted the readiness of the room — the bunk made up, the logs stacked beside the fireplace, the canned goods lined up store-neat, and the kerosene lamp with wick trimmed and waiting.

He blew on his hands to warm them, then picked up a log and whittled chips for kindling. He shook some kerosene over the kindling and laid on two logs. Lighting the fire, he cackled in relief as the flames leaped up.

The heat felt good to Brighty, too. He gave himself a violent shake, spraying snow over the entire room.

"Get away from me, you wet rat!" Irons swung around and struck Brighty with the flat of his hand.

The startled burro backed up, his hindquarters pushing against a door that squeaked open. Irons shoved him on through and peered into the darkness of a small lean-to. He grinned when he saw the little room was filled with logs. Not bothering to remove Brighty's pack, he stooped his way out, letting the door whine shut behind him.

Brighty paced restlessly in the blackness. He hungered for light and warmth, and most of all for food to quiet the pinching of his belly. He butted the door, then turned and kicked it. But suddenly he felt very tired, and his kicking was half-hearted.

A boot came crashing against the door on the other side, and a second boot, and after a while there were fainter noises — tin dishes clicking together, the slurping sound of soup and coffee; and after many minutes, a watch being wound, followed almost at once by a steady snoring.

When the trembling in Brighty's legs had quieted, he peeled a log with his teeth, slowly chewing the bitter bark. Then he nosed carefully along the wall, trying to find the green logs. Halfway around, his muzzle touched something that gave to his bunting. He bunted it again. The thing was rough-textured, and it made a rustly noise. He remembered that noise! Oats! Exquisite oats! With a grunt of joy he ripped a hole in the gunny sack, and then his muzzle was in among the plump kernels.

A pleasant feeling flowed into him as his grinders made meal of the grain, and the juices in his mouth turned it into a delicious mush. He lipped another mouthful and another, and after a while he stopped eating, his small belly satisfied.

A warmth surged through his body. With his forefeet inside the bag, in the snug little nest he had made, he too slept and snored.

Thief's Plunder

WHILE BRIGHT ANGEL SLEPT, the warm comfort spread all through him and he forgot he was trapped. But when he awakened, he stared about in panic. Even in the darkness of the lean-to his time sense told him it was morning. He cried out for his freedom, screaming and pawing.

On the other side of the door Jake Irons sat bolt upright, surprised to find himself in a bunk. He got up, rubbing his sore muscles, and hobbled stiff-legged to the window. All was whiteness. The sea of snow billowed away to a shore of snow-frosted trees, and the trees swept up the snow-veined slope to puffs of white cloud. But off to the north the sky was beginning to pink.

Irons rubbed his hands together, and his smile was a gash in his beard. His lips moved, forming the words "Utah! Utah!" He turned from the window and set to work, stirring the fire, piling on more wood. Meanwhile the noise in the shed grew more insistent.

"Shut up, you flop-eared fool!" Irons shouted as he thinned the flapjack batter.

Brighty heard the cakes drop into the fat with a sizzle and his nose caught the sweet smell. With one mighty kick he crashed through the door, wood splintering in all directions.

The two creatures wheeled around to face each other. In the awesome silence that followed, the man seemed to stop breathing. Then the dark anger in his face changed to cunning. "If I didn't need you to break trail," he bit off the words, "I'd whack this skillet over your head. Now back up, you shaggy brute. After I've et, I'll give you the leavings."

But Brighty stood his ground, stood watching while the cakes were turned.

"I s'pose," the man sneered, "you'd like yours all doused in honey and cooled, so's not to burn your pretty pink tongue." He squinted his eyes until they were slits. "Well, maybe there won't be none left!" He stacked his cakes four deep and drenched them with molasses until it dripped from the plate. Then he ate his way fiercely through the stack. At last, unable to swallow more, he set the leavings before Brighty, who nosed them a long time before he could stomach the taint on them.

While Brighty ate, Irons' hands and eyes were busy. He removed the burro's pack and opened it out so that he could add new plunder. Last night he had been too tired to investigate the big box he had pushed against the door. Now, eager fingers unfastened the lid and greedy eyes peered in. A jacket lay on top. Off with his mackinaw, on with the jacket.

Next he lifted out a pair of small-sized boots and held them up, squawking, "Wouldn't you know it? A runt of a man!" He threw the boots across the room in disgust.

Brighty picked one up in his teeth and shook it as a dog would. Then he sat down, letting the boot lean against him.

The bearded face was back in the box. Like any pack rat, the man was trading: a good felt hat for his ragged one, a pair of wool socks to be worn as mittens in place of his work gloves, another pair of socks for his own holey ones, some soft doeskin moccasins for his worn shoes.

Then back in the box again, hands seeking more — feeling in among the folds of a blanket, feeling and finding a smooth leather case. With a shout of discovery, Irons lifted it out and unsheathed the beautiful rifle. Hungry hands slapped the polished stock, slid a testing forefinger against the trigger, then along the shiny barrel, then back again to the stock, now fingering the gold plate.

Stealthily the man looked toward the window and then over his shoulder, as if he expected someone to be watching.

"Only broomtail!" he whispered. Turning his back so that even Brighty could not see, he held the stock up to the light to make out the wording.

Eyes unaccustomed to reading spelled out the letters one by one: "T-O J-A-M-E-S O-W-E-N F-R-O-M H-I-S F-R-I-E-N-D T-H-E-O-D-O-R-E R-O-O-S-E-V-E-L-T."

For an instant he looked at the shininess of the plate, then he pulled out his pocketknife and loosened the gold screws. With a quick motion of his arm, he flung the plate into the fire.

Now he moved more slowly, taking care not to forget anything — the coffee and the canned goods, the box of matches on the mantel. He packed the load on Brighty, lashing down the pots and pans and stolen things, all but the rifle. He tried to tighten the cinch, but Brighty blew himself up.

"I hope you bust!" Irons spat out the words as he gave a mighty tug. "Tonight I'll be rid of you. I'll be in Utah. And then . . ." His voice was a mocking singsong. "Then I'm just an innercent beaver trapper come to sell my skins."

He poked the muzzle of the rifle into Brighty's flanks, and with a laugh drove him out of the cabin.

In the Kaibab Forest

A WINDBLOW OF FRESH SNOW lay on the path they had tramped the night before. Making new tracks, Brighty stretched out his neck and moved gaily along. The good oats, the night's rest. and now the thin, crackly air made him feel frisky. Even the heavier weight of the pack was easy to bear. He tossed his head, snorting and squealing, and he tried a little dance.

Jake Irons' voice exploded like a machine gun. "Act your age! Git moving! No monkey business now!"

The frozen snow crunched to Brighty's feet as he wound his way between the blazed trees. If he made a right turn now, he would face Bright Angel Point, and beyond it the trail plunging away into the canyon. If he turned sharply to the left, he would come to a remembered ranch where cattle grazed and where there would be salt chunks to lick . . . Without hesitation Brighty charted his course for the ranch.

Irons, a stranger to the Kaibab Forest, glanced anxiously at the sun, to make sure they were headed north. Satisfied, he scuffed along, his moccasins following silently in Brighty's hoofprints, his new rifle pointed skyward.

The way humped over hills and dipped into hollows, and the forest marched in close with the littler pines in front. There was no path to see or to smell. Only the trackless ocean of white. Yet Brighty's sense of direction and his memory hurried him along.

In silence the two moved onward, each busy in his own mind. Once Irons stopped to tighten the ropes around Brighty's belly and to scoop up a handful of snow. Then they were off again, now out in the open, now swallowed by the forest, where only thin blades of light knifed their way through the gloom.

They saw no living thing. The deer had long since taken flight to lower altitudes, and even the mournful croaking of the ravens was gone. Brighty and the man were alone, two insect dots crawling through the vast stillness.

The sun climbed higher, and Brighty squinched his eyelids to wink away the glare on the snow. They passed mountain meadows bedded down for winter, and groves of quaking aspen staring at them with black-bole eyes. Midway of each rise they paused, sucking in deep draughts of the air and blowing out clouds of steam. Then on again, topping the rise only to see the land swell and stretch endlessly away to the north.

Presently Brighty was nosing the way excitedly. Some pygmy had made queer little prints in the snow, a lively fellow! So great were his leaps that his hind feet landed well ahead of his tiny forepaws. Brighty followed the elfin trail until it ended at the base of a pine tree. And there, high up, he spied the elf — a white-tailed squirrel that lives only in the Kaibab Forest. He was a plump young one, clinging to the tree like a cub to its mother. His body and the shine in his eyes and even the tufts of his ears were black, but his tail was a luminous white plume against the trunk.

Using the plume as a parachute, he landed on a lower limb and sat holding onto his perch, watching cautiously. Suddenly there was the sharp crack of a rifle, and the body of the squirrel arced into the air. It crumpled and fell kicking to the snow. Brighty watched the man pick it up and spin it by the tail. And the next he knew, the warm thing was added to his pack and flapping against his side.

Brighty nosed a green cone the squirrel had dropped. He paused to eat it, but the rifle poked him on, jolting the cone from his mouth.

In the little time it had taken to kill the squirrel, the sun slid behind a cloud. And now the sky was gathering up more clouds and smoothing them out into a gray hood over the earth. The wind lifted and made spindrift of the snow, so that Brighty had to purse his nostrils to keep it out.

He hurried along, his direction instinct sharpening. Soon now he would hear calves bawling and cows mooing and men's laughter. Over another knoll and another, and suddenly it was there — the friendly ranch house, snug inside a cup of white.

Leaving the man far behind, Brighty galloped toward it, churning the snow as he ran, pots and pans clanking. Any moment now a bunch of cows would come lumbering at him. Any moment now the door would fly open and men would hobble out on their cowboy heels.

He slid to a stop as he reached the house, almost falling down in his eagerness. He pressed his nose against the window, but saw only a cavern of darkness. He went to the door, pawing it, braying at it, waiting, listening. And then he heard a bellowing behind him. It was Jake Irons shouting, "You dunce! I give you hot cakes and biscuits, and you leave me behind to freeze and die!"

He broke off abruptly as a gust of snow showered him. A night's shelter would be best, he thought, and on to Utah tomorrow. He tried the door, opening it a crack, letting the rifle nose in first. Nothing happened. Full of bravery, he pushed it wide and strode in.

Brighty followed, his hoofs skidding across the smooth floor.

The Voice Inside the Snowman

THE TWO-STORY RANCH HOUSE was as deserted as a schoolhouse on Saturday morning. Men and cattle were gone, far away to House Rock Valley. Except for an old wooden cupboard, the place stood empty. There were no bunks, no table, no chairs. Just the old cupboard against the wall and a gaping fireplace with a bed of white ashes.

Irons, his rifle leading, walked through the emptiness and up the ladder steps to the second floor.

Here too was a chill air of desertion. The only movement was the snow swirling against the window.

He backed down in a hurry to find the burro pushing his nose against a heavy door at one end of the room. It hung on double hinges, and Brighty, with a little foretaste of pleasure, was butting it open.

Eagerly, Irons darted around him and struck a match to see what the room held. "Jerusalem!" he gasped, squinting at the pinkness. One whole wall was piled high with pink salt in hundred-pound chunks. Already Brighty's tongue was at work on the nearest one.

The opposite wall was stacked with logs, and up against them were a roll of wire and a hatchet whose blade winked in the matchlight. Irons started for the hatchet, but the flame sputtered and burned his fingers. With an oath, he picked up logs and hatchet in the dark and groped his way out, letting the door swing against Brighty's rump.

Carefully he laid his rifle on the deer horns fastened to the cupboard. Then he went to work, hacking chips from the logs. "Utah! Utah!" his lips kept saying with each stroke.

He smiled at how neatly everything was working out. "I got plenty of grub," he was thinking, "a warm place to bunk, and then Utah by noon probably." "Yeah," he said aloud, "better to stay here tonight and crash a new town by day."

While the logs were taking fire, he brought out Brighty's pack, and next explored the cupboard. There were three odd-shaped sacks in it — one containing a few potatoes beginning to sprout, one apples wrinkled and dried, and the third some kind of herbs or seeds. There were tin cups, too, and plates.

Together his supplies made quite a little pile, and he decided on a hearty meal. He'd have tomato soup to start with, and then fried squirrel and potatoes, and for dessert, coffee and apples, sugared. As he drooled in anticipation, he could hear Brighty peeling strips of bark in the salthouse.

"Eat hearty, broomtail!" he laughed, pulling out his knife and skinning the squirrel. He chopped the carcass into four pieces and dropped them in a skillet of sizzling fat. Meanwhile he heated the tomato soup and gulped it down. Then he sat rocking on his heels, watching the bubbles of fat boil up over the meat. He swallowed often, hardly able to control the juices that flooded his mouth.

Outside, in the black night, the snow masses struck down at the ranch house, enfolding it in a thick blanket.

Irons ate until there was only the back of the squirrel left. He stuffed it in the empty soup can and placed it near the fire. It would make a good snack later on. At last he spread his blankets on the floor and rolled himself up, feet to the fire.

When his snoring had become steady, Brighty came nosing into the room for food. He found a mound of potato and apple parings, and ate them slowly. With a curl of apple peel still dangling from his mouth, he went back to his salthouse to munch it. Then he too fell into a deep sleep.

Gradually the fire burned low, and cold crept into the house. Irons reached for a log and added it to the fire. For a long time he lay staring at the flames licking around it. Sleep was just beginning to claim him again when suddenly the outside door flew open and a cold blast of snow struck him in the face.

A shrouded figure broke through the mist. It was made of snow, humped and padded with snow, and its feet were chunks of ice.

Jake Irons lay rigid, as if strapped in his blankets. Was this some ghost out of his dreams? Some crazy shadow of the night? The figure couldn't be real. It was cloud-stuff, whipped up by the snow —a snowman with coals for eyes. The heat of the fire would melt it and would leave only a puddle of water with two dead coals swimming in it.

But the voice inside the snowman cried out, "Uncle Jim!" And again, "Uncle Jim! You here?"

"Git out!" Irons yelled. "Ain't no Uncle Jim here."

The sunken coals shone unafraid, and the snow-mittened hands that drew a hunting knife were unafraid. "I'd as lief die fighting as starving," a boy's high-pitched voice cried out.

Irons saw the blade of the knife threatening. He measured the distance to his rifle and the nearness of the knife. He got up, his lips curling in a make-believe welcome. "Come into my parlor," he said with a grand gesture.

At the same instant the swinging door opened and a pair of long ears and curious eyes peered around at the newcomer.

"Brighty! It's me — Homer! Homer Hobbs." The boy's voice caught in his throat. "Remember? You used to pack water for me!" He ran stumbling toward the burro and fell with his arms around Brighty's neck.

Irons kicked at a log in disgust. "The sobbin' fool!" He spat out the words. "Let 'em hole up together. Tomorrow I'll be rid of 'em both."

Trapped by the Snow

THE SNOW FLOWED ON AND ON steadily all night. By morning the three creatures were locked in a white prison. The ranch house was no longer a fort; it was a jail, and the jailer the snow.

Jake Irons paced in front of the window, hands clenched behind him. The windowpane was barred — barred and crossbarred by the snow. The tiny flakes were driving him mad. They were really nothing but froth. He could take a handful and crush them. He could shoot them with his rifle into splashes. Yet they laughed in his face like millions of guards, holding him, handcuffing him to a burro with eyes all-knowing, and to a greenhorn boy with frostbitten feet.

He turned from the window and deliberately stomped on Brighty's tail, as if he were responsible for the storm. With a howl of pain the burro scrambled to his feet, humping his hindquarters toward Irons.

The man broke into a laugh of scorn. "See that, kid? Your Bright Angel can't kick no higher'n a cricket any more. His spirit's broke. You'll get that way too, boy, livin' on nothin' but air." He squinted his eyes at Homer, trying to peer through his sweater to see if a silver star were pinned beneath. "Look-a-here, fellow," he said in a wheedling voice, "what's a young punk like you doin' in the forest this time of year? Hmm?"

Homer was rubbing his feet, wincing at the pain. "I been offered a job as lumberjack," he said, his voice low.

"Where at?"

"Across the canyon to Flagstaff."

"Whyn't you take it?"

"The blizzard caught me," the boy answered, still rubbing his feet. "I couldn't find the way. Been wanderin' for days all over the mountain." He swallowed hard. "I shoulda listened to Uncle Jim . . . I shoulda listened . . ."

"Quit your brayin'!" Irons exploded. "Not one, but two jackasses in this-here cell. Now who's this Uncle Jim?"

Homer looked up in surprise. "Why, everybody knows Uncle Jim. Even — "

Irons came a step toward the boy and shouted, "Answer me! Who's Uncle Jim?"

"Uncle Jim," Homer said earnestly, "is the lion-killer sent here by the government." In his mind he saw the gentle face, gray eyes smiling under the black hat. "He's a mountain man and canyon man, and he knows weather and lions and buffalo."

"And burros too, I s'pose."

"This one for sure. He saved Brighty's life — two, three times."

"Where's he at?" Irons shot his question.

"He's holed up for the winter, back in Fredonia. Oh, I shoulda listened . . ."

"Don't begin that brayin' again."

"Last words he said was, 'Wait till spring, Homer. Only Brighty could smell out the trail now.' "

Jake Irons curled his lip. "Brighty — Brighty — Brighty!" He snatched up the rifle. "If you don't quit makin' an angel outa him, I will!"

Homer sprang up, forgetting the pain in his feet. He pulled out his knife.

Irons laughed deep in his throat. "Can't take a joke, can you, kid? One minute you're a snivelin' sissy, and the next a wildcat. You make me sick. If I was to kill anyone, it'd be you. Burros only bray."

He scratched his beard with a dirty hand. "Now you're here, you can nurse yourself. Plenty of snow water to guzzle, and some apples as wrinkly as your gran'ma's face. Me, I practically lives on no food at all, 'specially if it's apples. They bloat my stummick."

He threw a log on the fire and wrapped himself in his blanket, the rifle beside him. "Might as well sleep out the storm," he mumbled to himself.

With Brighty tailing him, Homer limped to the door. Snow had sifted in over the threshold, and he swept it together with his hands and swallowed it. He went to the cupboard next and took an apple and ate it all, chewing up core and seeds too.

As soon as it was gone, he felt mean and selfish. He went back for another, this time giving half to Brighty. He stood watching the burro eat, and felt good for the sharing.

Satisfied, Brighty buckled his knees and eased down on his side in front of the salthouse. He wriggled and squirmed, trying to get comfortable on the hard floor. The boy crossed the room and settled down back to back against the burro. He sighed, enjoying the warm animal smell. It was good, and comforting too, to be near Brighty again.

He let his eyes wander sleepily about the room, and they lighted on the rifle. "Y'know," he mused drowsily, "Uncle Jim had a fine rifle like that one. Teddy Roosevelt gave it to him, personal. Only his had a big gold plate with writing on it."

Irons' nerves tightened. He sat up, scrutinizing Homer's face in the firelight. Did the boy know? Had he known all along? Then a wave of relief washed over him as he saw that Homer was simply talking himself to sleep. He watched the blond head sink deeper into Brighty's shaggy coat. He watched sleep come, and when the boy's arm thumped heavily to the floor, Irons got up and dug into the mound of ashes at the edge of the fire. His hands found the tin can, slyly pried open the lid, and pulled out the back of the squirrel, warmed to taste. He looked at it a moment, and then the gold teeth set to work tearing off bits of flesh. When the meat was ground and swallowed, he cracked the bones and sucked them, and at last he crunched and ate them too.

"Homer!" he barked, wiping his beard. "Wake up and feed the fire!"

Alone with the Night

SNOW! NEVER-ENDING SNOW! Wave on wave it sifted down, slantwise and spirally, dusting its fine white powder over the Kaibab Forest.

Morning came and night, and morning again — and still it fell. Stealthily the white mass crept up the sides of the house. It piled thickly against the window, filling the space between the bars, blocking out the light.

The three creatures were buried alive by the gray-white mass that wheeled out of the sky and made night of day. The cupboard now was completely bare, except for the useless bag of seeds.

Brighty alone had something to eat, but there was a hollowness inside him that the bitter bark could not fill. He drew away to himself. By day he took refuge in the darkness of the salthouse, and there he stayed, dozing some, nibbling some on the logs, and licking the salt for comfort. But mostly he stood in a stupor, head down, tail tucked in.

Only at nightfall did he come out of his hermitage and join the others at the fireside. Then, with his eyes climbing the ladder to the hole in the ceiling, he brayed to the night. It was as if he saw moon and stars instead of black emptiness.

The first time Homer heard him, his voice fell to an awed whisper. "I've a ghostly feeling," he said, "that Brighty's sendin' off some kind o' message."

The dire sound and the regularity made Irons' flesh creep, for each evening as the bray started up, he would take out his watch and check the time. And each evening it showed exactly five o'clock. Shaking his head, he would slide the key into the face of the watch and slowly wind while Brighty's cry faded away.

"Who you figger broomtail'd call to?" Irons asked one night as he returned the watch to his pocket.

Homer's eyes grew big. "Could be the living," he said. "Or could be the dead."

"Like, f'rinstance . . . ?"

"Like an old prospector he used to know, or maybe Uncle Jimmy Owen."

Quick hatred leaped into Irons' eyes. His fist swung out and struck Homer a blow that sent him sprawling across the floor boards.

The boy was too stunned to move. He watched in terror as Irons came slowly toward him, sharp canine teeth biting down on his words. "Don't mention neither of them two again! Never!"

There was a deathlike silence as Brighty slow-footed his way to the salthouse and the two men were alone with the night. Alone in the forest with the snow tightening around them, and no sound but Brighty gnawing on the wood, stripping it, grinding it, and then silence again, and the watch . . . ticking, ticking, ticking.

The two occupants had divided the room as sharply as if barbed wire reached across the middle of it. The half nearer the fire belonged to Irons, the half nearer the salthouse to Homer.

Now Homer huddled far into his corner, nursing his chin and his burning feet by turns. He tried to sleep, but his ear refused to shut out the relentless ping of the seconds. Suddenly he leaped up and ran into the salthouse, coming out with the roll of wire and a piece of old canvas.

A cold glint came into Irons' eyes. "What you doing? Figuring on escaping? Alone? Eh, kid?"

Homer turned a brave face to the man. "No! No! I'll make you a pair too."

"Pair o' what? Wings?"

"Snowshoes."

Irons' hollow laugh shattered the quiet. He sat cross-legged in his blanket to watch, his narrowed eyes on Homer's fingers.

The boy talked nervously as he shaped the wire into frames. "I'll make 'em beaver-tail style. No, they'd be too hard to handle in deep snow. I'll make 'em like a bear's paw."

When four frames were roughly shaped, he began tearing the canvas into strips for the webbing; but the effort exhausted him, and he fell back on his blankets, too tired to go on. By now Irons had fallen asleep sitting up, chin resting on his chest and unkempt hair hiding his eyes. Homer was relieved to be free of their fixed gaze. He tried to sleep too, one hand tucked inside his shirt for warmth, the other on the hilt of his hunting knife.

Brighty slipped up, unheard, and nosed him. Homer reached out to stroke the shaggy neck, and so, comforting each other, they both dropped off to sleep.

Mist wrapped itself about the house, and there was a heavy and ominous silence within. Terror shot through Irons' dreams. "Got to get out of this coffin," he mumbled. "Window's blocked. Door's blocked. Soon the window upstairs. No food left. Starving . . . starving. Listen, the watch! It knows more than it tells. Break it! Break it! Break it!"

Homer, worn out with fatigue, slept on while the frantic voice kept talking to itself.

"Starving! Starving! Got to get out of here. Listen, it's a time clock! Tick . . . tick . . . tick. It knows the hour of death. Closer, closer. The clock's going off . . . Break it!"

Irons woke to his own voice. Drenched in sweat, he threw off his blanket and picked up a chip of wood, lighting it for a torch. He saw that the boy still slept, lying against Brighty. His eyes studied the burro as if he'd never seen him before, weighing the meat on the ribs, counting the mouthfuls.

He used the chip as a poker to stir the fire, then with sneaking feet crept across the room, his trigger finger working. The thump of a loose floor board woke Homer.

"Don't move, kid." Irons' voice was coldly quiet. "Else I'll have me two carcasses to stew."

A slow, sickening horror came into the boy's face as he caught the meaning of the words.

The cold voice went on, "Name of Bright Angel's going to fit now. Not much meat. Tough and stringy, but I'm . . ."

He brought the gun to his shoulder and pointed at the wide space between Brighty's eyes. Then a small sound arrested him. Without his willing it, the hand that held the rifle froze.

Strange Thanksgiving

THE SOUND CAME AS SUDDENLY AS LIGHTNING — a tumbling, onrushing sound. It wasn't the wind growling in the chimney. What was it?

Homer and Jake stared at each other, their eyes asking questions. Some mountain lion scraping her claws against the upstairs window? Some white bat of a snow spirit beating its wings?

Homer was out of his blanket, facing into the muzzle of the rifle, but all senses, save his hearing, were numbed. He was struggling to bring in the strange sound. Brighty's ears too worked, swiveled, listened.

There! It came again, sweeping in closer. And all at once it exploded in a fury of noise — glass cracking, crashing, splintering to pieces. Then an eerie silence, followed by footfalls thudding across the upstairs floor.

Irons wheeled around, aiming his rifle at the ladder. He waited fearful, waited for something to happen.

It came quietly, like a raindrop from a tree long after the rain has ceased. Down from the hole in the ceiling, down the ladder steps, came a frail, wraith-like figure. It was feathered with snow, and the head and shoulders were quilted with it. Midway of the steps it stopped, and the eyes threw off glints like blue ice under the white shag of brows. Now the voice of the snow specter shattered the quiet. "Point that rifle down!" it commanded.

Irons obeyed, hands shaking, mouth suddenly gone dry.

The man facing him was little, almost puny, and his voice mild. Yet there was something in the eyes, a terrible courage and power which gave him command. The eyes were wide now, trying to believe what they saw. Unmoving, the little man stood there, halfway of the steps, erect under an enormous pack, and looked down on them all.

No one made a move or a sound. Not a welcome shouted, nor a bray. Not so much as a throat cleared.

In all that silence Brighty tiptoed soundlessly toward the steps, ears swinging free, eyes gazing up in recognition. He felt out the first step, the second, and on up until he could reach with his nose and touch the mittened hand.

"Bright Angel!" the man whispered.

Eyes held each other an instant. Then Brighty began an excited wheezing. The bray was a long time coming, but when at last it burst free in a trembling *"Eeee-aw! Eeee-aw!"* it flooded the room.

Now Homer was like a boy not wanting to be outdone. "Uncle Jim!" he cried out. "Oh, Uncle Jim! I knew you'd come!" His voice cracked. "I shoulda listened to you!"

Uncle Jim was carefully backing Brighty down the steps. "Shush, Homer," he soothed. "I'm the one's to fault. If I'd had a lick o' sense, I'd hog-tied ye till spring."

Irons, still holding the rifle, looked on in a trance. He watched the slight figure drop his pack on the floor and stamp the snow from his feet.

"Me and Homer's pappy used to drive buffalo," Uncle Jim explained, studying the rifle and the face above it. "Be a lot o' answerin' to do if I hadn't found his boy."

Irons' eyes wavered under the steady scrutiny.

"Got to frettin' about Homer, I did," the old man went on. He pulled off his sealskin cap and slapped it against the fireplace. "I figgered the boy'd never make it. Likely as not I wouldn't neither if I hadn't knowed every inch o' this-here forest. Now, stranger," he said, taking a step toward Irons, "you know my name; I'll have to ask yers."

"Jake Irons." The words were out before the man could stop them.

Uncle Jim looked down at the moccasins and up again at the sinister face as he pelted his questions hard and fast.

"Where you come from?"

"The canyon."

"How come ye got Brighty here?"

"He wanted to come."

"Humph!" Uncle Jim snorted his disbelief. "Where be ye headin'?"

"To Utah, to sell my beaver skins."

"Funny about that," the quiet voice went on. "Most trappers hugs the canyon in wintertime, and then sells their pelts come spring."

"I do it different." Irons bit his lip and hatred rose in his face. "See?"

The air tightened, was suddenly fraught with suspense, but the little man was still master. "Where'd ye get it?"

"Get what?"

"I'll ask ye just oncet more." He pointed to the rifle. "Where'd ye get it?"

"What's that to you?"

"Talk fast, Jake Irons," Uncle Jim said, pulling out his six-shooter. "Homer'll tell ye I kin drive nails with this li'l ole notched piece."

Irons' eyelids slitted as he stepped back a pace, groping for an answer. "A trapper I knew. Yeah, a trapper; he give it to me."

"Hand it over," Uncle Jim said very quietly.

Irons was a man hypnotized. His breath came hard and fast. He tried to stare back at the fearless eyes, but his own refused to focus. They faltered, then fell on the six-shooter being returned to its holster and the gnarled old hands reaching out for the rifle, and suddenly taking it!

"Hm . . . mm." Uncle Jim was a long time looking at the scarred place where the gold plate had been. He decided at last not to reveal his discovery. "Reckon I made a bad blunder," he said, glancing sidelong at Homer. "Thought it belonged to a friend, but his was summat different."

Relief spread over Irons' face as Uncle Jim laid the rifle on the cupboard. Brighty heaved a sigh, as if he too had come through a tense moment.

"You fellers mayn't know it," Uncle Jim changed the subject, "but this here's Thanksgiving, and we're goin' to have us a feast. But first off, Homer, you trot upstairs and tack somethin' over that winder I broke. And fetch down my snowshoes so they kin thaw out. Irons, you stoke up that fire and put a lot o' snow water to boil."

Sitting on the floor, Uncle Jim pulled off his boots and five pairs of stockings, one at a time. A pair of red socks remained on his feet.

"Brighty," he said, rocking back on his hands and scratching the burro's belly with his stockinged toes, "it's a long night since I seen you! Three years and a mite more!" He gave Brighty a quick smile. "I'm glad you come back, feller, and there'll be no questions asked."

Brighty nudged Uncle Jim for more scratching, but the old man saw hungry eyes looking at his pack, and he got up to open it. Wrapped inside the blankets were a side of bacon and small sacks of flour, sugar, coffee, and raisins. Uncle Jim poured a little sugar into his hand and offered it to Brighty.

"Lord-a-mercy," he said, as the burro lapped it up. "Ye're ribby as a washboard; it pinches me inside just to look at ye."

He wiped his hands on his pants and busied himself with supper. "Somebody's et squirrel meat," he said, smelling the skillet and wrinkling his nose. "Me, I don't like my vittles mixed." He handed the pan over to Irons. "Heat it red-hot, man, and burn the charred mess out o' it. Then scour it clean with that old burlap sack.

"Now, Homer," Uncle Jim turned to the boy, who was angling the snowshoes against the fireplace, "you add a handful o' lard and two o' snow to this flour, and then beat it a hunnert licks. More if yer strength holds out."

A feeling almost of coziness came into the room — Homer stirring the batter, Irons burnishing the frying pan, and Brighty bunting Uncle Jim just to keep reminding him of their reunion.

While the biscuits were baking, Uncle Jim made a wick from strings of the flour sack and dipped it in a small can of lard. "I likes to see what I'm eatin'!" he pronounced as he lighted the makeshift candle. A bright arrow of flame shot upward, and the bare room seemed transformed.

Homer snuffed the mingled odors of bacon frying and coffee boiling and the lard candle. "Smells mighty nice, Uncle Jim. I been living on nothin' but apples and snow water for days."

While the three men sat eating by candlelight, Uncle Jim's eyes were on Brighty. "Mebbe," he thought, "I'll have to wind saplings around his feet like little round snowshoes. No," he shook his head, "might be all right for horses in Iceland, but not for Brighty." His gaze went down to the tiny hoofs, and he could see them plunging through the crust on the snow and thrashing about in a wild panic to be free. He shuddered. "I'll puzzle this out some way," he promised himself.

When Brighty too had eaten his biscuits and a handful of raisins, Uncle Jim turned to Irons. "Me and you'll wash up," he said, "while Homer works on his snowshoes. 'Pears to me the webs is too far apart. With more crosspieces, they won't be so saggy when they gets wet."

Brighty footed his way to the salthouse. Later Uncle Jim took the candle and looked in on him. "Jumpin' kangaroos!" he exploded. "Never seed a critter so neat nor two men so lazy! I'll be danged if he ain't mounded all his jobs in one corner and here they be, frozen and ready to pitch out. Yet ain't a hand done fer him!"

Moon Lily Tea

When all the dishes were put away in the cupboard and the salthouse cleaned, a hush spread over the room. Homer was working on his snowshoes, and Irons sat staring into the fire, screening his face from the others.

Uncle Jim broke the silence, chuckling. "Now't our bellies is plumb full and everythin's nice and tidied," he said to Brighty, "let's me and you cozy up fer the night."

He spread his blankets on the floor, and sitting down he pulled off a stocking and drew it back and forth between his toes. "Here I be, feeling good and noble-like," he sighed, "just 'cause I made a li'l ole jack happy. Don't it beat all how righteous a feller feels after doin' a li'l muckin' out!"

Uncle Jim expected no answer and got none. He wriggled down into his blankets and lay on his back, laughing up at Brighty, who kept circling him, trying to make up his mind where to settle. "Y'know, Bright Angel," he said, "this is the first time I ever see ye in yer winter coat, and it sure is frowsy. Ye got woolly curls on yer forehead, and over yer eyes it looks 'zackly like a thatched roof. Don't it, fellers?"

"Sure does," Homer agreed, as he interlaced the canvas strips of his snowshoes.

Irons grunted in this throat at all the talk of Brighty. He got up to get more wood, and as he passed, the burro shied out of reach.

"Hey!" Uncle Jim raised up on one elbow. "Why's Brighty so skittish o' ye?"

Jake Irons did not answer at once. "Why . . . uh," he floundered at last, "he's jumpy from being starved. Same as me. Yeah, that's it."

The old man's jaws clamped, and his hands made sure of the six-shooter by his side. He turned now to Homer and saw the weary flush of the boy's face. "Quit workin', son, and blow out the candle. Tomorrer's another day. Lemme see," his voice went drowsy, "we got chuck to last three, four days. Then we got to light out, for better or worser."

Homer and Irons bedded down in their corners, with Uncle Jim and Brighty on the imaginary dividing line. Quiet again filled the room, save for a small, steady ticking. And then, just as Homer's lips made an O to blow the candle, Irons took out the gold watch and began winding.

Uncle Jim's heart started knocking against his ribs. The room suddenly seemed to contract. There was nothing in it but the gold watch, like some meteor flashing out of the past. In his mind's eye he was down in the canyon, seeing Old Timer with the same watch, winding, winding, winding. Old Timer's murderer here! In this very room — a big, bold, easy target.

The ticking grew louder, like a hammer striking on steel. Uncle Jim flattened his back to the floor, his hands feeling for the revolver. He remembered the sheriff's promise: "We'll capture 'im — dead or alive."

"Dead!" Uncle Jim's lips formed the word. "Dead it'll be!" His fingers tightened on the gun, and as he began pulling it out of the blanket he felt a squirming at his back. It was only Brighty settling closer, but the movement jolted the old man's thoughts. "Who'd be the murderer then? Who? Me! Uncle Jimmy!" And he thought, "Death's too easy. He's got to atone. Me and Brighty'll pack him out alive!"

He saw the watch now held to Jake Irons' ear, saw it returned to its pocket, saw him cover himself with a blanket strangely familiar and get ready for sleep.

"Them li'l pin eyes!" Uncle Jim thought. "Pack rat's eyes!" His mind began pacing back and forth. Suddenly it pounced on an idea, and he reached around, patting Brighty as if thanking him for the interruption.

"It'll work!" he said to himself with fierce determination. He waited until his angry trembling was over and his breathing steadied. Then into the silence he forced a belch. It was a big gusty belch, and it was followed by another, even louder.

"My stummick's kind o' queasy-like," he said, throwing off his blankets. "That bacon grease seems to o' gagged me. Guess I'll brew up a pot o' Moon Lily tea. I recollect seein' a packet of pods."

He went over to the cupboard to get them. "Ye all just lay there and I'll give ye some when it's done." He opened the outside door a crack, filled the coffeepot with snow, and set it over the fire.

"The Piute Indians thought a heap o' Moon Lily tea," he went on, his breath slow and even now. "Used it for the stummick and other troubles. Wisht we had us some canned milk, but it's flavory even this way."

He remembered to belch again, and then he made a great racket setting out the tin cups, to be sure no one fell asleep. "Either o' ye fellers feel sick?" he asked.

"Not me," Homer said.

When the tea was ready, Uncle Jim handed a steaming cup to Homer and one to Irons. Then he sat down alongside Brighty to sip his own.

"Get yer nose out o' this," he laughed. "This here's one thing ain't good for man *and* beast."

"Why, it tastes nice," Homer pronounced. "And to think it was here all the time!"

Irons gulped noisily and set the empty cup on the floor.

"It's a queer thing about this Moon Lily tea!" Uncle Jim said. "The Piutes had a great use fer it asides fer the stummick." He interrupted himself with a belch. "Now take, f'rinstance, if some thief stole a hoss . . ."

"What then?" Homer asked.

"Then," Uncle Jim said, "they'd find a way to get

a cup o' this-here tea into 'im, and in a little while the tea'd loosen his tongue and he jest couldn't stop blabbin'. He'd tell 'zackly where he stole that hoss and where he'd hid it."

"Honest?" Homer asked, and added, "I'm glad I ain't stole nothin'." He hesitated. " 'Cept once I took some overripe peaches out of a orchard down to Fredonia."

"By thunder!" Uncle Jim slapped his leg in delight. "Ye're still guzzlin' yer tea and already ye're confessin'! The Piutes used to say, 'Big crime take longer.' "

There was a moment or two of silence before Uncle Jim pointed his revolver at Irons and asked, "How 'bout ye, Jake? Tea beginning to sweat out any thievin' or killin'? How about a murder? Y'ever hear o' Old Timer?"

Irons choked, and his face went purple-red. The questions were striking into him like barbed arrows. He tried to get up, but he only writhed in his blankets, hands held against his stomach. "I been poisoned! I been poisoned!" he screamed. "It was Old Timer's fault! His own fault!" The words poured out in a torrent. "He was there on that ledge and I aimed to pass, and his footing give way and he fell — splash — into the river."

"And p'raps" — Uncle Jim's voice was slow-measured — "p'raps his footing give way 'cause you pushed him? Just a leetle? Eh, Irons?"

Irons' voice shrilled. "No! No! No! 'Twas only a little nudge I give him, and he made a death scream and he was bobbin' in the water like a piece of wood, and then he got sucked under."

"You awake, Homer?"

"Yes, Uncle Jim."

"Willing to be my witness, Homer?"

"Yes sir."

"And so ye stole his watch, Irons?"

"He hadn't no need for it! The sheriff came, and another old coot, and I warn't going to give them the watch."

"That other ole coot was me, Irons."

Terror caught at the man. He tried to stop his lips with the back of his hand, but the tumble of words rushed on. "That Old Timer," he shrieked hysterically, "could've kept his old rocks. They never paid off."

Uncle Jim's eyes were cold and mocking. "Now ain't that just too bad. Here I thought 'twas a nice big vein, like the one bulgin' on yer forehead."

Irons clasped his head. "No! No! No!" His voice rose to the breaking point.

"That rifle," Uncle Jim demanded, "where'd you throw the gold plate on it?"

"In the fire! In the fire!"

"At a cabin back a ways in the meadow?"

The man screeched his "Yes."

Still holding the revolver on Irons, Uncle Jim walked backward, skirting around Brighty. He took his own rifle off the cupboard and gave it to Homer. "We'll have to stand watches on this scoundrel," he said to the boy, "till we can hand him over to the law. As fer ye, Jake Irons, one move and that loose clapper o' yer tongue will be stopped fer good."

As Homer took the rifle, a change came over him, an almost man-grown look. He pointed it at Irons and settled himself, ready to shoot.

"By the way," he asked after a while, "how's your stummick feel now, Uncle Jim?"

For answer the old man threw his arms around Brighty's neck and laughed into the shaggy hair. "Moon Lily tea, me eye!" he chortled. "Them weren't any lily pods. I gave ye real green tea what I packed along from Fredonia!"

No Escape?

THE SNOW CONTINUED TO FALL. For four days more it piled up. Now only the rooftree and the chimney of the house were uncovered. Inside, the feeling of desperation grew. The tunnel of the wide porch had seemed a last avenue of escape. Now it too slowly closed in.

Three pairs of snowshoes against the wall, waiting. The men and the burro grown thin, waiting. Flour almost gone. Even the candle grease eaten.

And now hunger gnawing, hurting, and morning and night stalking each other, and Old Timer's watch sounding big in the quiet.

With the windows sealed, the air grew foul. Homer called out in his nightmares. "Uncle Jim! Uncle Jim! I can't breathe! They're clampin' the box lid down. They got my fingers caught. Save me, Uncle Jim. Save me!"

Even Brighty slept fitfully. He took to nightwalking. From salthouse to hearth, from hearth to salthouse, back and forth, back and forth, until Irons' nerves too were breaking.

"Stop him!" he screamed at Uncle Jim. "I'm going crazy! Stop him!"

"Humph!" Uncle Jim snorted. "You been crazy all along, crazy as a hoot owl, thinkin' to get away from the law." He shook his pistol like a forefinger. "A quick, outright killin' is too nice fer the likes o' ye. There's got to be a trial with eyes boring into ye and questions spit at ye, and ye a-sweatin' and a-squirmin'."

A new idea struck him. "Or could be," his voice dropped to a whisper, "could be the snow's the law. Mebbe the snow's yer leg irons, holdin' ye down till ye starve to death."

Just saying the words and trying to make his voice sound big took all the old man's strength. He leaned against the wall to hide his exhaustion.

A crazed look came into Irons' eyes. "I ain't going to starve! I ain't going to die!" He reached under his blankets where he had hidden some raisins in a soup can. He popped one into his mouth and another, squashing them with his tongue, then chewing fiercely to get the full strength.

Without a word of warning, Uncle Jim drew a bead on the tin can and shot it out of Irons' hand. The man fell back, unhurt, on his blanket.

"What happened? What happened?" Homer called out in alarm.

"Nothin' much," Uncle Jim chuckled. "A rat was just makin' off with the last o' our raisins, and I sure scared the livin' daylights out o' him."

"I heard tell of starving people eating rats," Homer said.

"You nor me couldn't stummick this one, Homer. It was a sick 'un, enough to pizen yer blood. I missed him a-purpose." He relaxed against the wall and felt stronger for the sureness of his aim.

"Uncle Jim?" A pink flush crawled up Homer's face to his temples.

"Yup?"

"Supposin' we don't make 'er out of here?"

"Ye're talkin' foolish now."

"But just suppose."

"All right. I'm supposin'." He looked at Homer and saw that the boy seemed overcome with what he had to say. "What is it frets ye, son?"

"It's just . . ." Homer's voice faltered. "I wanted to tell you . . . I'm sorry."

"Pshaw. I knowed ye was. Knowed it all along. But hadn't been fer ye, we might never o' catched Jake Irons, nor had us this reunion with Bright Angel. I'm tired now, boy. How'd it be if ye stood watch fer a bit?" The old man talked on, but his words were muffled in drowsiness as sleep overcame him.

The boy sat up straighter, his back against the cupboard, his rifle pointed toward the dark lump that was Irons.

Blazing Guns

HOMER SEEMED ALONE — all, all alone with sleep. He was shut in with sleep, and it was deep as the night is and long as the day is. The steady sounds of sleep came to him — Uncle Jim's a slow purring, and Irons' the harsh snore of a man lying on his back. But Brighty's was uneven, troubled perhaps by dreams.

As he kept his lonely watch, Homer's fingers played along the rifle, feeling the chill of the steel, feeling the four tiny holes where the gold plate had been. He rubbed the smoothly polished wood, and his thumbnail made an imaginary notch.

"I could do it now!" he said to himself, and a fierce joy leaped up in him. "I could kill Jake while Uncle Jim sleeps. I could pull the trigger.

It'd be easy. Just one little pull, and then I could sleep too."

His forefinger slid around the trigger guard, then fitted itself into the curve of the trigger. He raised the rifle and took aim. A shadow leaped up on the wall. It was the barrel of the rifle, a finger accusing. "Coward!" it said. "Coward!"

Homer tried to ignore the pointing finger, but it sidetracked him without his willing it. He looked at Uncle Jim and thought of his gallant courage. How little he seemed, and old! And the forelock of his hair was all of one color with Brighty's — a dusty gray, like sagebrush.

The thought of sagebrush set Homer to longing for summer winds and summer skies, and he forgot he had intended to kill a man. He shrugged at the shadow on the wall, and with a sigh lowered the rifle.

The fire licked its way around the logs, and one log fell with a shower of sparks. Blue vapor curled and rose, and the boy watched the flames, letting his ears listen for trouble.

But there was none. Only the fire making little crackles like squirrel feet running on dry leaves. And the sleep sounds — deepening, slowing.

Homer's eyelids began to droop. He blinked rapidly, trying to focus on the objects in the room.

He picked out his snowshoes and made believe they were magic. He could put them on and walk off across the snow to a table set with chicken legs, and he would gnaw them clean as if he were a dog, and then he would suck on the bones. But the table faded away, and in its place he saw nothing but snow — downy, drowsy snow, drifting gently down.

The gauzy stuff enfolded him, whirled him slowly around, until he was sucked up and up into a cloud. And the cloud was made of feathers of sleep — so restful, so restful. He cushioned his head in their soft comfort, and his eyelids closed.

Minutes wore on. Then in the quiet Irons stirred. The ratty head of hair poked out of the blanket and the pin eyes glanced sharply around. They saw Homer's chin resting on his chest and the rifle lying clear of his hands.

A quick scheming and hunger for revenge distorted Irons' face. He threw off his blanket and, dragging it behind him, stole across the floor. He tried not to hurry. A creaking floor board could give him away. He eased toward Homer, keeping close to the wall, not wanting his footsteps to be heard or his scent to reach the burro. And then, in two spurts against the firelight, Brighty's ears came up tall and stiff. There was no time to lose. From where he stood, Irons flung the blanket over Homer's head, and suddenly he was on top of the boy, his right hand snatching the rifle.

Homer thought it was the cloud smothering him, and he awoke, fighting off the blanket, crying out in terror, "Uncle Jim! Uncle Jim!"

But Uncle Jim, pillowed on Brighty, lay helpless. Jake Irons stood towering over him, the bore of the rifle aimed straight at him.

"So you wanted to see *me* squirm!" The gold teeth showed in a savage grin. "Now who's scairt and sweatin'?"

Uncle Jim looked out of sad, tired eyes and forced a little smile. "Not me, Irons. Likely ye'd be doin' me a favor."

"O.K., old coot. Here's your favor!" And Irons pulled the trigger.

There was a flash, an explosion, a scrambling of feet, and then a heavy thump. When the smoke cleared, the dark dribble of blood that ran along the floor came from Brighty and not from Uncle Jim. Brighty's shoulder was stained with blood, and his head lolled backward, eyes wildly rolling.

Instantly Uncle Jim returned the shot. No sighting or bringing up of the pistol. Just one shot from the hip. Yet the aim at the rifle was sure — bead of steel delivered with cold, calculated fury.

"You done 'er, Uncle Jim! You done 'er!" Homer shouted as the rifle banged to the floor. "Look!" he cried, picking it up. "The loading breech is dented. Can't nobody fire 'er now! Look!"

Uncle Jim did not look at the rifle, nor down at Brighty. Not yet. He straddled the quiet body like a mare protecting her foal. Then with pistol held steady on Irons, he snapped out his orders.

"Homer! Pull the cupboard away from the wall.

"Irons! Squat down, yer back agin the cupboard."

The man slumped to the floor, a defiant leer on his face. He sat against the cupboard, motionless except for his eyes. "Only the pistol left now," he thought, "and the old man tiring." But his look of cunning gave way to surprise and then to fear as the clipped directions went on.

"Lash him to the cupboard with that-there wire! Bind him fast, Homer!"

The boy's awkward hands wrapped the wire around Irons, and around the cabinet too — once, twice, three times. Then he twisted the ends securely and stood up, waiting for the next command. It came without a word of reproof. The six-shooter, warm from the firing and from Uncle Jim's grip, was laid in his hands.

A Score to Settle

AND NOW AT LAST Uncle Jim was on his knees. He was no longer the general barking out commands, but a little stooped man whose knees cracked when he knelt and whose eyes were wet.

"Brighty!" he said softly. "It's me — yer Uncle Jimmy. Look at me, Brighty!"

The white lids opened, and the dulled brown eyes looked around until they found Uncle Jim.

"Please don't go under, feller. Not this-a-way. God's give me lots o' strength I can still do fer ye!"

In proof he half ran to the salthouse and brought back kindling and a log, and he fed the fire for light. He worked quickly, paying no heed to his own labored breathing. The pitchy wood crackled, and in the flashes of fire he saw dark blood pumping out of Brighty's shoulder with each heartbeat.

"Lemme have a look now," he said, forcing a note of confidence into his voice. Gentle hands laid back the bloodmatted hairs, little by little.

"It's only a flesh wound, Brighty, just below the cross on yer shoulder." But to himself he was crying, "It's all ragged and blasted out, and blood vessels pumpin' theirselves dry! I'm afraid, God."

Homer's voice cut in. "How bad is it?"

Brighty lay with mouth open, gasping for air. His shoulder felt sticky and hot and twisted. He heard the murmur of voices, but they were far off, like voices in a dream. He tried to lift his head, and the small movement spurted the blood.

"He'll go under, Homer," Uncle Jim looked at Brighty with fear, "less'n we kin . . ."

"Unless what, Uncle Jim?"

"Less'n we kin dam up that flowin' red river." The old man jerked to his feet, and headed for the salthouse. "We got to stop it! We got to!"

He snatched up the hatchet and began hacking at the floor inside the salthouse, hacking fiercely with every ounce of his strength. The hard-packed dirt loosened into bits and pieces. He raked them together with his fingers, praying as he worked.

Back with Brighty again, he was nurse and doctor, soothing, explaining. "This is clean dirt, feller. Been under salt. It'll work like a sponge." Carefully he eased the whole handful into the gaping wound, biting his lip and wincing at the pain he inflicted.

He watched the blood ooze and bubble darkly through the dirt. "Listen, Bright Angel!" he pleaded. "Ye can't leave me like this! You and me's got a score to settle for Old Timer. And when it's done, then 'twon't be a whisker o' time afore ye'll be lopin' down yer old trail and splashin' in Bright Angel Creek again. Seems like I can eenamost hear the creek callin' fer ye to come and play."

He stopped and was silent. He sat down beside Brighty, his eyes never wavering from the wound. Slowly the dirt pack did its work. By and by the bleeding ceased, and after a while Brighty's muscles relaxed and his eyelids closed. He slipped off to sleep, using Uncle Jim's knee for a headrest.

"Ye shouldn't o' come between," the old man said, as he stroked the furry ears. "I'm an old buck, Brighty. Ye shouldn't o' done it fer the likes o' me." He shook his head sadly. "My poor li'l wild 'un, all tuckered out."

There was no telling how long Brighty slept. Snowbound time has no seconds or minutes. It is an hourglass with snow for sand, and unseen fingers turning it. Uncle Jim slept too, while Homer watched his sullen prisoner. There was no more sleep in the boy. He wondered if he could ever close his eyes again.

Homer looked down at the pistol in his hands. Then he was suddenly looking at his hands. Something was happening to them, something which he could not stop. They were shaking. Now his whole body was shaking. "My grandfather shook like this," he thought in panic, "but he was old."

At the same moment a rumbling blast set the dishes in the cupboard to dancing and rattling. A new panic caught at him. "An earthquake!" he thought. His mind said the word and his throat shouted it, "Earthquake! Earthquake!"

In one confused instant the cupboard doors flew open, and tin cups, plates, and spoons came pummeling down on Irons' head.

Uncle Jim blinked at the crash. A furrow of puzzlement formed between his brows. Then suddenly his eyes were bright as meteors, and he was laughing and looking old-young again.

"Dynamite!" he shouted. "Someone's blasting the snowbank! They're comin' to save us!"

The Way Home

THE RESCUE TEAM of the sheriff and his young deputy had faced their errand of mercy with great courage. They knew well that finding Uncle Jim and Homer alive was extremely doubtful, with snow fifteen feet deep and temperatures below zero. Unless the old man and the boy had taken refuge in the ranch house or in Uncle Jim's cabin, there was almost no chance of finding them at all.

But Uncle Jim was so beloved by the whole town of Fredonia that everyone wanted to help. Housewives offered their warmest blankets, the postmaster contributed his mail toboggan, the harness-maker stuffed a straw mattress for it, and the storekeeper donated bacon, oatmeal, coffee and sugar.

Fortunately the deputy, remembering a story of arctic adventure, took along a few sticks of dynamite. Without them the rescuers might not have gained entry to the ranch house in time.

It was the smoke curling out of the chimney that told them someone was there. And as fast as numbed fingers could work, they set off the blast that startled Homer half out of his wits.

When they burst in upon the starving group, the sheriff was the one most deeply moved. Pleased as he was to see Uncle Jim and Homer, and even Brighty, he was astounded to learn that the man bound to the cupboard was the long-hunted desperado who had murdered his friend.

The sheriff buzzed like a bee in clover. He could hardly contain himself while Uncle Jim told about the Moon Lily tea and the confession. He whipped out his notebook and wrote furiously, as if each thrust of the lead were a stab in the flesh of Irons.

Then, with great officiousness, he turned to the prisoner. "In the name of the law and as sheriff of

Coconino County, I arrest you, Jake Irons," he said pompously, "for the murder of one Hezekiah Appleyard and attempted murder of one James Owen."

In spite of his eagerness to deliver the criminal to justice, he could see that Uncle Jim and Homer, and Irons too, would have to be fed and strengthened for the trip.

Uncle Jim pretended a great weakness in order to give Brighty time to recover. "It's my legs!" he complained. "They're rubbery as them toy knives kids play with. But lemme see now . . ."

He went over to the burro and washed the dirt from his wound. With a glow of pride, he noticed that the blood vessels were already sealed and the tissues a brilliant red. "In my next life," he thought, "mebbe I could be a horse doctor instead o' a lion hunter!" Out loud he said, "Sheriff, with all them vittles ye brung, I reckon my legs'll be stal'art as ever by day after tomorrow."

"No need to use your legs," the sheriff replied. "That's why we got the toboggan. You can loll on it like a mermaid the hull way home."

Uncle Jim was not listening. His mind was at work. Day after tomorrow! Only two days to ready Brighty! He began pacing, as if that would help help him think. He paced around the deputy and Homer, who were busy getting supper, and around the sheriff, who was going through his prisoner's pockets. At last Uncle Jim had the schedule worked out in his mind.

In the two days that followed, his only thought was for Brighty. He made him hot mashes of rolled oats and fed him sugar for energy. He poured bacon grease, lukewarm, into the wound. Then, in half-hour stretches, he walked Brighty around in a circle, like a groom tuning up a race horse for a big event.

The sheriff guffawed. "For one who's got rubbery legs," he said, "yours is mighty spry." Then he winked at Uncle Jim in understanding.

Morning of the second day dawned bright and clear. The sun threw a glitter on the snow, and the sky arched deep and blue. Shadows of deeper blue slanted out of the timber and sharpened the white of the snow.

A party of five men with a toboggan was making its slow way across the freshly varnished world.

"Just take 'er easy, fellers," the sheriff said, his breath making a column of steam in the air. "The snow's got a good crust, and the pines'll show us the way home." He began laughing. "It this ain't a comical sight! Here's a parcel of people footing it, and the beast of burden riding!"

Uncle Jim, paddling like a pelican, lifted one web foot over the other. "Don't see nothing so hilarious to that," he said tartly. Then he took in the sight — Jake Irons wearing a harness and pulling the toboggan with the burro aboard. He began to grin. "Reckon it *is* a thing at that!"

His eye was on the straining figure, but what he really saw was little Mimi, using the reward money to buy one of the newfangled wheel chairs and scooting around in it faster than if she had good legs. He saw Old Timer's watch dangling from the arm of the chair, and Mimi prizing it above everything.

"Sure it's funny!" the sheriff roared. "Oddest rescue I ever seen!" He poked his gun in Irons' ribs. "Today's easy," he said. "Tomorrow you'll be weighin' in on the scales of justice."

Snowshoes creaking, the party tramped onward, Brighty's blanket a red splash against the whiteness.

"It's a wonder our lung pipes can stand the shock o' fine fresh air," Uncle Jim said after a while.

"I can't suck in enough of it," Homer said breathlessly. "You reckon Brighty can take it?"

Uncle Jim's face clouded. He watched the slight, blanketed figure brace itself as Irons floundered up a rise. "Mebbe," he thought in sudden alarm, "the thin cold air is too much for him, him being weakened and all, and this his first winter away from the canyon."

And then, almost at the top of the hill, Brighty's head came up and his ears forked sharp against the sky. It gave the old man a start to see the sudden change. It was as if a frisky young jack had taken the place of a tired old one.

"Why, he looks spunky!" Uncle Jim smiled to himself. "He's just a li'l ole youngster been cooped up too long and is addled with freedom!"

It was true. Brighty had changed. He seemed aware all at once that he was free — no one gripping his tail or prodding him with a rifle, and no walls hemming him in. The wide, free world and the sky above were his! He tossed his head, testing and tasting the air, letting strength flow back into him. The red blanket began rippling, then billowed to the movement of his lungs. He tried a little whinner in his throat, and it grew bigger and wilder, and came out as of old — a steam-whistle bray, high and joyous: *"Eeee-aw! Eeee-aw! Eee-aw-aw!"*

Uncle Jim, too, took in a great lungful of air. "Brighty ain't goin' under!" His voice cracked in happiness. "Yup, fellers, he's goin' to make 'er!"

And the rocks and hills rang with the words. "Yup, fellers, he's gin' to make 'er!" they shouted again. And then again.

AND NOW . . .

Canyon winds still blow restless. And the Colorado River still cuts its way, depth upon depth, through the mile-high walls. And from the far corners of the world men come to explore this open book of the earth's crust. Some are scientists and other artists, and some are troubled people who come to find themselves, to drop their worries into the great chasm.

Riding muleback, they zigzag down the face of the wall, over some of the very trails marked out by Brighty's feet. Often in the middle of the descent their mules come to a dead halt, long ears lopped over a ledge, eyes sighting a tiny lone fellow far below.

Then up from the distance a piercing voice calls: "*Eeee-aw! Eeee-aw! Ee — aw — aw!*"

"Look!" the guide cries. "Down yonder — a wild burro! Maybe," he grins to the riders behind him, "maybe it's Bright Angel!"

Of course everyone knows that Brighty has long since left this earth. But some animals, like some men, leave a trail of glory behind them. They give their spirit to the place where they have lived, and remain forever a part of the rocks and streams and the wind and sky.

Especially on moonlit nights, a shaggy little form can be seen flirting along the ledges, a thin swirl of dust rising behind him. Some say it is nothing but moonbeams caught up in a cloud. But the other guides swear it is trail dust out of the past, kicked up by Brighty himself, the roving spirit of the Grand Canyon — forever wild, forever free.

RANCHHOUSE
TO FREDONIA
KAIBAB FOREST
CLIFF SPRINGS
UNCLE JIM'S MEADOW
ROARING SPRINGS
DEVIL'S BACKYARD
RIBBON FALLS
PHANTOM CREEK
BRIGHT ANGEL CREEK
BRIDGE
COLORADO RIVER
TONTO PLATEAU
TO SOUTH RIM
N
W
E
S